INTREPID ANGEL

As Liz Archer exited from the hotel, Clay Hammet stepped forward into the street. She spotted him and stopped cold.

"Angel Eyes!"

"Don't do this, Clay," she said.

"I'm gonna prove it to you, this town and to Toliver. I'm the fastest gun there is."

"Clay, this is wrong. There's no need for one of us to die.

"Hah! You're scared."

"I'm afraid, all right – afraid that I'll have to kill you."

Peripherally she became aware of some commotion in another part of town, but she dared not take her eyes off of Hammet.

ANGEL EYES

#6

BULLETS AND BAD TIMES

Also by Robert J. Randisi

Angel Eyes

#1: The Miracle of Revenge
#2: Death's Angel
#3: Wolf Pass
#4: Chinatown Justice
#5: Logan's Army
#6: Bullets and Bad Times
#7: Six Gun Angel
#8: Avenging Angel
#9: Angel for Hire

Tracker

#1: The Winning Hand
#2: Lincoln County
#3: The Blue Cut Job
#4: Chinatown Chance
#5: The Oklahoma Score

Mountain Jack Pike

#1: Mountain Jack Pike
#2: Rocky Mountain Kill
#3: Comanche Come-On
#4: Crow Bait
#5: Green River Hunt

ANGEL
EYES

#6

BULLETS
AND
BAD TIMES

Robert J. Randisi

SPEAKING VOLUMES, LLC

NAPLES, FLORIDA

2012

ANGEL EYES

#6 BULLETS AND BAD TIMES

ISBN 978-1-61232-588-0

To all the Hacks

Don't let anyone tell you it's bad!

CHAPTER ONE

Liz Archer pulled the collar of her fur-lined jacket higher, a futile attempt to keep the chill of the Dakota Territory off the back of her neck. This was the farthest north she'd ever been and she was starting to think that maybe her subconscious had known something, keeping her away from this region as long as it had. Montana had been bad enough, but this. . . .

Absently she patted Blossom's neck. The mare, unlike her mistress, seemed to relish the cold weather. Farther back a sign had said the town of Clearwater was five miles ahead. Liz couldn't wait until she reached it. It seemed to her that they had travelled more than that already, and she began to squint and crane her neck in anticipation of seeing the town.

God, she hoped she'd be able to get some rest in Clearwater. Lately it seemed she had either been getting drawn into other people's fights in one way or another, or simply dealing herself in. For some unknown reason she couldn't seem to keep out of trouble. Maybe she just couldn't help herself, like that time in San Francisco. That had not been her fault at all. And then there was that episode in Wyoming, but she couldn't very well leave the Carters to fend for themselves against hired guns, could she?

Tate Gilmore, the man who had taught her to use a gun, had done so only after telling her that her life would never be the same again. Once she started using her gun, he said, trouble would have no difficulty finding her. In spite of the warning she had gone after the men who had killed her family and her fiancé, and ever since then she and trouble seemed to ride the same trail.

Maybe this time it could be different. She decided to mind her own business this time.

That was for damn sure. . . .

Clay Hammet was twenty-two and impatient.

Hammet had grown up in the area, and after the death of his parents when he was seventeen he'd moved into town, making his way by doing odd jobs. Eventually he'd begun to do some jobs for the town gunsmith, and he'd become fascinated by all kinds of guns. After that he had made a bargain with the gunsmith to do any and all work for him as long as the man paid him by letting him practice with the guns in his shop.

Since then he'd become lightning fast with a gun, and he thought that he was faster than anyone.

Some folks might have said he was impatient to die, but *they* didn't realize how truly fast he was with a gun. Clay himself knew that he was faster than anyone alive or dead, including Hickok. Lord how he wished that Hickok was alive today, or that Tate Gilmore was riding into town, but he was apparently going to have to settle for a woman — although not just any woman. The one they called "Angel Eyes" had made herself a reputation in a relatively short period of time. Clay Hammet planned to make his even faster, and he was going to start with her.

Hammet couldn't believe his luck when he'd heard from a friend, via telegraph, that Angel Eyes was heading his way. He hoped she wouldn't bypass the town of Clearwater for some reason, but if she did he'd just go out and look for her.

He wasn't about to let this opportunity pass him by.

That was for damn sure. . . .

Sheriff Al Toliver sat wearily behind his desk, running his hands through his short-cropped gray hair. The weariness did not come from any physical exertion, and it seemed to be happening more and more of late. It might have had something to do with the fact that he'd managed to cram eighty years of living into fifty. More than likely though, it now had to do with the fact that Liz Archer, the woman they called Angel Eyes, was heading toward Clearwater.

That meant trouble. It always did when those kind of people showed up.

Toliver chuckled ironically to himself as he thought, sure, *those* kind of people. How long ago had it been that he had also been one of *those* people?

In his earlier days Toliver had been a hellraiser, a

youngster with a quick temper and an even quicker gun hand. He'd started to carve out quite a reputation with a gun until the day a little girl — to this day he couldn't remember her name — ran between him and another man in a hurry to die, and got herself killed.

It had been the other man's bullet that hit her, but the incident still had a profound effect on Toliver. After that he was no longer anxious to build a name for himself with a gun. He'd seen in the young mother's eyes the kind of grief a gun could bring. He decided right there that rather than bring more grief into the world, he'd use his life to try and keep as much of it as he could out of the world.

He became a lawman.

So Al Toliver had lived two separate lives on both sides of the law, but he'd been one of the lucky ones. He'd gotten smart early, and as a result he was still alive. True, from time to time it had been necessary for him to use his gun to achieve his goal, but to this day he'd killed less men in the last twenty-five years of his life than he had during his three years from age twenty-two to twenty-five. He was proud of that but felt that very soon he might be put sorely to the test.

He knew Clay Hammet. In fact he saw some of himself in Hammet and had hopes of getting through to the boy and turning him around. He had even offered to make the boy a deputy, but Hammet had laughed — a snide, derisive laugh that said plainly what he thought of lawmen. The arrival of Angel Eyes, however, could change all of that. If she killed Clay Hammet, or even if he killed her, the boy would be lost to Al Toliver.

He didn't know how he was going to do it, but he was going to keep Clay Hammet and Liz Archer from facing each other with their guns.

That was for damn sure. . . .

When Clearwater finally came into view Liz Archer had no idea that there were two men in that town who were anxiously awaiting her arrival.

If she had known, things might have ended differently.

CHAPTER TWO

Liz's first desire upon nearing Clearwater had been a hot bath, followed by a hot meal, followed by some sleep. That had been before Blossom had started to limp, having picked up a stone bruise on her left front hoof. First thing she'd have to do now was get Blossom put up and give her time to heal. After that, whether or not the town was a good place for Liz to rest, she'd have to stay there until the mare was ready to travel again.

She put Blossom up at the Clearwater Livery and pointed out the bruise to the liveryman.

"Do you have a vet in this town?"

The liveryman lifted Blossom's hoof and examined the injury. Having done that he gently put her hoof back on the ground and stood up. He was a man in his forties and was tall and broad shouldered. He squirted some tobacco juice before speaking.

"You don't need a vet, miss. I been around horses all my life. I know just what to do for her." He put his hand on Blossom and Liz could see the gentleness of his touch. "She'll be fine."

"I'd be grateful, and I'd pay you."

"No need," he said, waving his hand and hesitating long enough to squirt once more. "Just pay for her feed and keep, the rest is free. She's a fine animal, be my pleasure to care for her."

"I'm much obliged," Liz said. She obtained directions to the Clearwater Hotel then and left Blossom in the man's apparently capable hands.

As she registered at the hotel she asked the young clerk about the availability of a bath. Apparently, the thought of Liz Archer naked in a bathtub on the premises completely tongue tied the clerk, who was about twenty and had an Adam's apple like a doorknob.

"A bath?" she asked again.

"For Chrissake Clem, tell the lady what she wants to know."

Liz turned her head in the direction of the voice and saw a tall, handsome man in his thirties standing about five feet to her left. He had apparently come down the steps from the hotel's second floor and heard her request.

"Oh, yeah, sorry," the clerk said. "We got a room in the back, ma'am, with two tubs."

"Hot water?"

"Yuh, I can get that for you."

"I could get it for you too, if you like," the other man said. She looked at him again and he was smiling a wide, white-toothed, cocky smile that said he knew he was attractive to women and this one would be no exception.

"Do you work in the hotel?"

The man removed his hat and said, "Hal Charles is my name ma'am, and no I don't work for the hotel. Fact is, I'm a guest, but I'd still count it as a real honor if you'd allow me to tote your bath water for you. I'll even clean your back if you like. I'm a real good back cleaner."

"I'm sure you are, Mr. Charles —"

"You can call me Hal."

"— but I think I'll settle for the clerk getting me my water. That's his job," she said, ignoring his attempt at more familiar terms.

The man looked confused for a moment, and then put his hat back on and walked out. It was probably the first time a woman didn't faint dead away at the sight of his smile, but she was sure his ego would survive.

"I'd like to put my saddlebags in my room. Would you get that bath ready for me?"

"Uh, sure, yes ma'am, right away!"

"Thank you," she said, flipping him two-bits.

"Yes ma'am," he said, and watched longingly as she walked to the steps and started up. When she was out of sight he snapped into action and hurried to get her bath ready. Before doing so though, he looked at the name she had signed in the register. His Adam's apple bobbed madly as he read the name a second time, and then he knew that drawing her bath would have to wait.

He hurried out from behind the desk and ran across the street to the sheriff's office.

Clay Hammet was with Dolly, his favorite of all the girls in Zelda's House of Entertainment. Dolly was his age, and she managed to make him feel as if he was the best man she'd ever been with.

Dolly was a tall, willowy brunette, with small breasts and slim hips. She had buttocks like a boy's, but she had a real pretty face and a wide, full-lipped mouth that she knew how to use real good.

She was using it on him now as he lay naked and spread-eagled on her bed, but for once he was thinking of something else while he was with her. He was thinking of the moment he would face Angel Eyes. He could see himself drawing and firing, catching her with her gun still in her holster, and he imagined that the crowd of onlookers would gasp at how fast he was.

Dolly chose that moment to fondle his balls and suddenly he was spurting into her mouth just as he mentally pulled the trigger again.

"Wow!" Dolly said appreciatively, sitting up on her knees and looking at him. "You like to took my head off that time, Clay."

"Sorry, Dolly honey," he said, "but you was really good, that time. *Really* good!"

The door to his office banged open and Al Toliver looked up to see Clem, the hotel clerk, staggering toward his desk.

"What's wrong Clem?"

Clem's huge Adam's apple jumped up and down disconcertingly as he struggled to get the words out.

"She's here, Sheriff!" he finally managed to say. "She's here!"

"Who's here, Clem? Come on now, calm down and tell me what you're all het up about."

"She's here! That gal you said you wanted to know about. She's here, in the hotel. She just checked in."

"You mean Angel — I mean, Elizabeth Archer?"

"That's how she signed the register."

Toliver sat straight up in his chair.

"What did she say to you?"

"Nothing, she checked in and asked about a bath. I'm supposed to be getting it ready, now."

"All right," Toliver said, rubbing his hand over his rough-hewn jaw. "All right Clem, you go over and you get that bath ready, and you let me know when she's in it. You hear? The minute she's in it!"

"I hear ya, I hear ya."

"All right, now get back there before she misses you."

"Right."

As Clem left his office and hurried back across the street Toliver stood up slowly, trying to shake the weariness that had settled into his bones.

Well, she was here. He wondered where Hammet was and if he knew yet. With a little luck he'd get to her before the boy did and persuade her to leave town. Maybe she'd be reasonable. If not, then maybe he'd have to be a little more forceful.

CHAPTER THREE

Liz settled into the steaming hot water prepared to bake the weariness from her body, but as soon as the door opened she was aware that someone was entering the room.

Her gun and holster were hanging within easy reach on the back of a straight-backed chair next to the tub, and she languidly stretched one arm over her head, hoping to sufficiently mask her next move.

"No need to go for that gun, Miss Archer," a man's voice said.

For a moment she wondered if it was the man from the lobby — was his name Hal? — but the voice was too low and steady to be his.

"In case you're wondering," the voice said, coming closer, "my name's Toliver, Sheriff Al Toliver."

He came into view then, to her left, and before she realized what he was doing he had reached for the chair bearing her gun and moved it so that he could sit in it, placing himself between her and her gun. He was a stocky, solidly built man with slate-gray hair and eyes, probably in his early fifties, although he wore it quite well. His eyes, she noticed, looked very tired, and he hadn't shaved.

"Sheriff, are you in the habit of visiting ladies in their bath?"

"No ma'am, but then it isn't everyday I get Angel Eyes in my town."

"Well," she said, sliding down into the water and relaxing a bit because at least she knew what it was about now, "that was fast."

"Somebody with a rep like yours can't travel without being noticed, Miss Archer. I knew you were headed this way, and I was hoping you'd bypass Clearwater, but I've been waiting for you, in case you didn't."

"And now you'd like me to clear out."

"Yes."

"Why — or is it for the obvious reason?"

"Which is?"

"That a person like me creates trouble, or carries it along?"

"I'll tell you the truth, Miss Archer," he said. "There's a young fella in this town who fancies himself a gunman. In fact, you aren't much older than him, but I suspect you're a lot more experienced."

"In killing people you mean?"

"I didn't mean —"

"This young man have a name?"

The sheriff nodded.

"Clay Hammet. Now, you wouldn't know the name and a lot of other people wouldn't know it either, but he thinks you can change that."

"Me. How?"

"By dying."

That's what she thought.

"Sheriff, believe it or not, I'm not looking for trouble."

"That may be, but he is."

"Then go and talk to him about it, not me."

"I have talked to him, and I will again, but I want you to leave town, Miss Archer. It's the best thing for everyone concerned, believe me."

She was tempted to sit straight up as if to comply with his request right then and there, and see if the sheriff embarrassed easily or not, but she decided not to play that game with this man.

"Oh, I do believe you, Sheriff, and I wish I could help you."

"You won't leave?"

"I can't," she said, and explained about her horse being lame.

"That'd be Jed at the livery," he said, rubbing his hand over his jaw. "He's got a real fine hand with horses. Your mare will do better with him than she would with a vet."

"That's fine, but how am I doing with you?"

He looked at her then, and she felt it was the first time he was looking at her as a woman and not as a bad reputation that had found its way into his town. She dropped a bit lower into the bath so that the water level was touching her chin.

"I wouldn't make you leave on foot or leave your horse behind," he finally said.

"I appreciate that, Sheriff, I truly do."

"You can wait for your horse to heal, but then you've got to leave."

"I will, I promise. I told you before, I'm not looking for trouble."

"I'll have a talk with Clay," he said, and she noticed that he called the young man by his first name. "Maybe I can talk some sense into him."

"He's not kin to you, is he?"

"Kin? No, he's just . . . very much like someone I once knew," the sheriff said, standing up. He seemed about to leave but then, as an afterthought, moved the chair back to where it had been giving her easy access to her gun again.

"Thank you."

"I'm sorry I interrupted your bath."

She searched his face for a trace of embarrassment but found none.

"That's all right. I understand."

He touched his fingers to the brim of his hat and left her to her bath.

The water had cooled off by now, so she lathered up, rinsed off, and stepped out, drying herself. The door started to open again and she made what could have been a fatal mistake, assuming that it was the sheriff again.

"Did you forget something?"

"I surely did," Hal Charles said. He was smiling,

but it wasn't as cocky or charming as it had been in the lobby. As he closed the door behind him the smile on his face was downright nasty — as was the gun in his hand!

"What are you doing here?" Liz asked.

"That should be obvious," he said, licking his lips. "You weren't very nice to me in the lobby, and I'm giving you a second chance."

"Save your energy."

He scowled and said, "Drop that towel, bitch." He wasn't nearly as attractive or as charming as he had been down in the lobby.

"Mister," Liz said, feeling absolutely no fear of the man, "if you think I'm just going to give up so you can rape me, you're mistaken."

"Lady, I got the gun," he said, reminding her, "now drop that towel."

Her own gun was on the back of the chair, which was an arm's length in front of her. She knew she could get to it in time, and if it hadn't been for her conversation with the sheriff she wouldn't have worried about killing this fool. The range was right, and the man certainly didn't look like a gunman. If her mentor, Tate Gilmore, ever found out about this. . . .

"All right, friend," she said, "I'll drop the towel."

Instead of dropping it though, she tossed it and it fell toward the floor, revealing her pale, full breasts with their pink nipples, distended from the chilly air that was wafting over her. The man's eyes popped and, as the towel fell between him and her gun, she reached out and snatched her weapon from her holster.

"Wha —" the man began, but whatever he'd been about to say was cut off by the sound of her shot.

The bullet plowed into his right shoulder, rendering his right arm and hand useless. His gun dropped to the floor and he slid down after it, clutching his shoulder and whimpering like a whipped dog. A flow of scarlet leaked out from between his fingers and dripped to the floor.

She had just enough time to get dressed and strap on her gun before the pounding on the door started. She moved forward using her foot to move the wounded man aside, and let in Sheriff Toliver, followed closely by the desk clerk.

"What the hell's going on?" Toliver demanded. His gun was in his hand and he was upset. She didn't blame him, but it hadn't been her fault so she offered no apology.

She indicated the man on the floor and said, "He wasn't as polite about interrupting my bath as you were."

CHAPTER FOUR

Toliver didn't just let her walk away, but it amounted to the same thing. He made her wait as he went over Clem's story again. The clerk had seen the sheriff leave and then had seen Charles sneak into the back. After that he'd gone for the sheriff, and they'd arrived just in time to hear the shot.

They waited while the doctor came with some men to help Charles to his office.

"When you're done with him, Doc, I've got a cell for him," Toliver said.

The doctor, a small, tired looking man in his sixties, said, "He'll need some rest."

"He'll get plenty," Toliver said, and then he told Liz to follow him to his office.

In his office Liz said, "You can't possibly blame me for this."

"Sure I can. Oh, I don't mean that you did it on

purpose, but you were there and that's what caused it."

"That man came after me because I was a woman, not because I'm . . . Angel Eyes."

Toliver's jaw assumed a stubborn jut, and then he relaxed and said, "You're right about that, but Christ, this is just going to make Clay even more anxious to go after you."

"Have you spoken with him yet?"

"I never had a chance, that fool Charles saw to that."

"I can't hide, Sheriff."

"I know, I know, damn it."

She felt sorry for the man. He obviously had some sort of bond with the younger man he was trying to protect, and he also had a job to do. She regretted that her presence was making it that much harder.

"I'm going to try and get a hot meal," she said, moving towards the door.

"Try the cafe down the street. Tell the woman there I sent you. Her name is Louise."

"Louise. Thanks."

"Do me a favor."

"What?"

"We've got two saloons. Clay usually goes to the Clearwater. If you want a drink, try the Metzger's."

"Metzger's? I'll remember."

"I appreciate your cooperation, Miss Archer."

"If we're cooperating," she said, "you can call me Liz." When he didn't reply she added, "And I'll just call you Sheriff," and left.

Louise turned out to be a sturdy woman in her forties

and, when Liz told the woman that Toliver had sent her, she could tell that there was something between the two of them — at least on the woman's part.

"Mind if I sit down with you, honey?" Louise asked after she had brought Liz's dinner.

Liz looked up in surprise and said, "Uh, no, not if your boss doesn't mind."

"Boss, ha! My husband owns this place and he don't mind anything I do."

So the woman was married, but still had eyes for the sheriff. Liz wondered what the sheriff felt. Louise was certainly a handsome enough woman — especially for someone in her forties — with dark hair, a full bosom and swelling hips. Unfortunately, she carried around just a little too much weight, which was probably not the fault of her age. Liz had a suspicion that the same condition probably existed when the woman was twenty.

"Just passin' through town, honey?"

"Yes."

"What's your connection with the sheriff?"

"No connection. He simply told me where I could get a hot meal."

"That's all?"

"That's all."

"Ain't interested in him, then? You know, as a man, I mean?"

Liz looked at Louise and said, "I just met the man, Louise."

"Yeah, but he's attractive, don't you think?"

Liz shrugged and admitted as much, saying, "In a gruff sort of way, I guess."

"Yeah, he's gruff, all right," Louise said, staring

over Liz's shoulder at nothing in particular, "but I'll get through that."

Liz couldn't resist asking her, "What about your husband?"

"What about him?" Louise McQuinn asked, a look of distaste coming over her face. "All McQuinn is interested in is this cafe and a bottle every night."

Liz wondered why so many wives referred to their husbands by their last names.

"How does he get along with the sheriff?"

"They're friends," the woman replied frankly, "which is why I'm having such a damned hard time with Al. I'll get through to him, though. He wants me, I can tell."

Liz nodded noncommittally, wishing she weren't so hungry and that the stew wasn't so good, otherwise she would have made an excuse and left.

As if reading her customer's mind Louise said, "Ah well, I'll let you eat. I got some more customers coming in. Thanks for letting me talk, honey. I don't get to do it, much."

"Anytime, Louise," Liz said, biting her tongue afterward and hoping that the woman wouldn't take her up on it.

"Let me know if you want something else, hear?"

"Thanks."

The woman went off to take care of her other customers and Liz was able to enjoy the remainder of her meal in silence.

The incident at the hotel didn't take long to get around town, and without a doubt the most interested citizen was Clay Hammet.

"Damn she's here!"

He was in the Clearwater Saloon and the bartender looked at him as he exclaimed, slamming his fist down on the top of the bar.

"Who's here?"

"Angel Eyes."

The bartender didn't need help recognizing the name. Hammet had been talking about her all week, ever since he'd heard she was headed this way.

"That lady gunfighter?"

"Yup."

"That's the one you been braggin' on, sayin' you was gonna plant her?"

"That's the one."

The bartender leaned his elbows and forearms on the bar and asked, "When you gonna do it?"

"First chance I get."

"Don't it bother you, Clay, thinkin' about shootin' a woman?"

"Not when I think about what it's gonna do for me, no sir."

"What's it gonna do?"

"It's gonna make me a name, Ed. It's gonna make me famous, like Hickok."

"You ain't as fast as Hickok."

Clay Hammet smiled at the bartender and said, "You wait and see, Ed. Everybody is gonna see, and real soon!"

CHAPTER FIVE

Sheriff Toliver found Clay Hammet just where he hoped he'd find him, sucking up whiskey at the Clearwater Saloon.

"Are you clear-headed enough to hear what I'm saying?" he asked, moving up next to the younger man.

Hammet looked at Toliver and smiled, sipping from the drink in his hand.

"Hey, my friend the sheriff." He gestured with his glass which, had it not been almost empty, would have sloshed out onto the lawman's clothes. "Hey, Ed, get my friend the sheriff a drink."

Toliver looked at the bartender and shook his head. The bartender moved to the other end of the bar.

"Hey, Ed —" Hammet started, but Sheriff Toliver

cut him short. "Come on," Toliver said to Hammet, taking hold of his right elbow, "let's get a table."

"Hey," Hammet said, yanking his arm away and finally spilling the rest of the drink he was holding, "that's my gun hand!"

"Then why do you have a drink in it?"

Hammet frowned at that one, then grinned and switched the half-empty glass from his right hand to his left.

"You thought I was too drunk to notice, didn't you, Sheriff?"

"At least you're too drunk to get yourself killed," Toliver muttered.

The sheriff and the would-be gunman sat at a table against a wall and Hammet finished his drink.

"Hey," he said when his glass was empty, "I forgot my bottle."

"Forget the bottle."

"How can I celebrate without a bottle?"

"What are you celebrating?"

"Angel Eyes," Hammet said. "She's in town, isn't she? Just like I been waiting for her."

"That's what I want to talk to you about, Clay."

"See, she is here. I heard she was here, but now you confirmed it." Pleased with the confirmation he said, "I gotta get a bottle."

"Forget the bottle!"

Hammet looked sharply at the sheriff, then grinned a drunken grin again.

"Oh, I get it. You think I'll go after her drunk. I won't go after her drunk, Sheriff. That'd be stupid. I'll go after her as sober as a sudge. I mean, jober as a judge — and it won't be right away, either. No sir. I'm gonna make her sweat a little, first."

"That lady is not going to sweat, Clay. Not over you, anyway."

"You don't think so, huh? Well, you wait and see," Hammet shouted. "Everybody just wait and see!"

Toliver saw that there was no talking to Hammet right then, so he bought the boy another bottle and waited while he consumed part of it. When Hammet finally fell over with his head on the table, snoring, Toliver tossed the boy's skinny frame over his shoulder and carried him to the jail where he could sleep it off — and where he could keep an eye on him.

On the way to the jail Toliver happened to pass Liz Archer in the street.

"Starting early, isn't he?" she asked.

"He's celebrating."

"Celebrating what? Is it a local holiday I don't know about?"

"Not hardly," Toliver said. "This is Clay Hammet."

"Ah," she said. She maneuvered around so she could see what he looked like. "You planning on keeping him drunk the whole time I'm here?"

"I hadn't thought of that," Toliver admitted, "but it is a pretty good idea. Right now I'm going to put him in a cell to sleep it off."

"Does that mean I can get a drink without worrying about him?"

"You can. He won't be a problem to anyone until

at least tomorrow. You, uh, gonna go into the saloon to get a drink?'' Toliver asked.

"Where else would I get one?''

"It's just that, you being a lady and all —''

"Why, Sheriff,'' she said, interrupting him, "I didn't think you noticed that I was a lady.''

"I noticed, miss. I would just appreciate it if you would sort of try and stay out of trouble. You know, a woman alone in a saloon — well, some men just sort of take that as an invitation.''

"I know what you mean, Sheriff, and I thank you for your concern. I'll be on my best behavior.''

"Well, I'd better get the boy to his cell for the night. I'll see you tomorrow.''

"Good luck with him, Sheriff,'' Liz Archer said, and continued on in the direction of Metzger's Saloon.

Keep him drunk the whole time, huh? On his way to the office with his burden, the sheriff actually gave that some serious thought.

CHAPTER SIX

When Liz entered Metzger's saloon she could feel the change in the air as most of the men in the place turned to look at her. For a brief moment she considered leaving and going to her hotel, but then she thought, what the hell, she was thirsty. She'd have one drink and leave before some drunken Romeo could get any ideas.

As it turned out the men in the place were obvious look-but-don't-touch types, and she decided to order a second beer, as well.

She took the beer over to a table where a poker game was in progress and paused to watch the four players. Charles Edward Taker — known as "Chance" Taker — a lover from her past, had been a gambler, playing cards to make his living. He had taught her to play poker, but she'd never made much use of the knowledge. Now as she watched she remembered all the rules and all the advice that Chance had given her. Instinctively she knew that the four men were not very good at what they were doing, and she suddenly remembered that her money was running low.

"Would you like to sit down and play, miss?" one of the men asked. The question drew him a dirty look from one of the other players, but the remaining two didn't seem to mind.

"You're welcome to sit in, miss," one of the others said. "It sure would be better if I didn't have to sit here with just these three ugly faces to look at."

"Well . . ."

"You do know how to play poker, don't you?"

"I know the rules, but I haven't played very much."

"We can show you," the first man said. "Go ahead and sit yourself down. The game is better with five players, anyway."

Especially one who was inexperienced, she thought. She had no doubt now that these men — three of them anyway — saw her as a sheep to be fleeced, and she was pretty certain she could teach them a lesson.

"All right," she said, pulling out the fifth chair, "I'll play."

She experienced an apprehensive moment when she withdrew her money from her pocket. She only had about twenty-five dollars left, but they didn't seem to be playing very high stakes.

That, she discovered, would come later.

In the beginning she seemed to win rather easily — by design, she was sure. They were drawing her in, trying to boost her confidence.

As they played she took the measure of the four men. All were in their thirties. The man who'd invited her to play initially was called Jake. He was tall and slender, had a pleasant enough face and fancied himself a card shark. He frequently riffled the cards before dealing, as if he were the only person who could perform the feat.

The man who had not been happy with the others' pick of a pigeon was short and muscular, and did not have the hands for playing cards. More than once the group had to change decks because he bent a card with his stubby fingers, and as the game went on she realized that it wasn't an accident every time. His name was Bull, and he was not a pleasant looking man — especially when he was unhappy, like now.

The other two were called Lee and Ben and she got the impression that they were brothers. Both were about six-foot with brown hair and eyes, and they had the same shape jaw and mouth.

Jake seemed to be the leader of the four and she noticed that the others watched him closely, as if waiting for some sort of signal.

She was fascinated, because she had learned the game from a skilled gambler, who had also taught her ways to cheat, just in case, and she saw that Jake was sloppily dealing seconds. The other deals all seemed to be on the level, perhaps because the others were not as adept as Jake with a deck of cards — and he was pitiful!

For this reason she did not feel any guilt over what she intended to do.

Gradually, as the game went on and she dealt a few times, she started to get the feel of the deck. Chance had often made her deal seconds until her hands hurt, and it was starting to come back to her. She would never have tried it with a pro, but these four were far from pros.

Once she had a decent amount of their money in front of her Jake made the offer.

"What do you say we raise the stakes a little, miss?" he asked. "You seem to have a lot of our money there."

They were referring to the two hundred dollars she had in front of her. It seemed odd to her that they would risk so much just to get her twenty-five dollars, but then she realized that they probably didn't know how much she had. Wouldn't they be surprised if they knew just how little they were working for?

"What do you say?" the man asked again.

She made a show of staring down at her money and then said, "Well, all right."

With a satisfied look on his face Jake began to deal. That hand was also won by Liz, but that was the end of the confidence building.

From then on she won a hand every so often, but only on the luck of the cards, and only when someone other than Jake was dealing. Her fortunes went up and down and when the time finally came for her to make her move, she was up about a hundred dollars, having given them back half of their investment.

The deal came to her and she quickly stacked the cards right under their noses, amazed at how easy it was. She knew that she had done it slowly and sloppily, but Jake, the self-professed card shark, had not even blinked.

She dealt out a hand of five card stud and watched

their faces as they read their cards. Jake seemed especially pleased and opened immediately.

"Ten dollars."

Bull and Lee called while Ben raised another ten. Knowing exactly what all four men had in their hands, Liz called the raise and the original bet, a total of twenty dollars.

"All right," she said, and asked how many cards each man wanted.

"Oh, I'll just play these," Jake said, holding the cards close to his chest.

"Pretty happy with those, aren't you?"

"They'll do."

Bull and Lee asked for three cards each while Ben took only one. Liz herself took three.

"It's your bet," she said to Jake, and he immediately bet twenty dollars.

Bull had bettered his hand to the point where he raised. Jake looked surprised when Lee raised, and then again when Ben raised. He look at Liz, expecting her to go out.

"I'll just call. This is a very interesting hand."

There was four hundred dollars in the pot, which certainly qualified as a lot of money to the four men, and she doubted if they realized that most of it was theirs. Jake looked at his cards, then raised again, giving the other three men meaningful looks.

"Fifty dollars."

"That's a little steep," Bull said, getting the message.

"I'm out," Lee said.

Ben, on the other hand, had such fine cards that he really didn't want to go out. So caught up was he that he raised Jake fifty, which drew him a look that might have been able to kill.

"I guess I'll call," Liz said, throwing the last of her money into the pot.

"I'm going to raise again," Jake said, and it was as if he was talking directly to Ben.

Ben got the message, looked mournfully at his cards, and then unwillingly went out.

"It's up to you, miss," Jake said, glaring at Liz Archer.

"Well," Liz said, "I guess I'll have to raise you."

Obviously surprised, Jake was nevertheless undaunted.

"I'll raise you again."

"Well," Liz said, looking at the table in front of her, "I don't have any more money, and I certainly want to call . . ."

"What do you mean, you don't have anymore money?" Bull demanded.

"I have a proposition for you, though, " she said to the one called Jake.

"What?"

"This one hand decides everything. If I win I take all of the money."

"Without seeing my raise?"

"I'll see your raise."

"With what?"

"With me."

He stared at her, and during the silence Bull said, "This is bullshit."

"Shut up!" Jake said. "What do you have in mind?" he said to Liz.

"If you win I'll go to your hotel room with you."

"Tonight?"

"Now, if you like."

"To do what?"

"Do I have to tell you?"

"I don't trust you," he said, licking his lips nervously. "I want to hear it exactly."

"I'll go to bed with you."

He leaned forward and asked, "You'll let me fuck you?"

"Absolutely."

"Jake —" Bull started.

"Shut up, Bull!"

Jake put his cards down on the table, revealing a full house, aces over kings.

"Missy," he said in an entirely different voice than he'd been using during the game, "I'm gonna make you so sore you won't be able to sit on a horse for a month."

"I don't think so," Liz said. She laid her own cards down and revealed four queens. "You lose."

As she raked in the money Bull looked at Jake and said, "You idiot! That was most of our poke!"

The two men glared at each other while Lee and Ben — to whom she'd dealt a straight to the jack — looked from one to the other with blank stares on their faces. Liz took the opportunity to pick up her winnings and prepared to leave.

"Where do you think you're going?" Jake demanded.

"I'm going to my room. I started out with only twenty-five dollars to my name and I want to thank you boys for your kind donations."

"You cheated!" Jake said.

"That sounds odd, coming from a cheater like you, Jake. You're probably the worst dealer of seconds I've ever seen. You did your best to boost my confidence so you could win all my money. What you didn't know was that all I had to my name was twenty-five dollars."

"Twenty-five dollars?" Bull exploded. "You said she had money!" he said to Jake.

"I said she looked like she had money."

."You stupid —"

"You ugly —"

"I'll just leave so you gentlemen can fight it out," she said, moving away from the table, "but my personal opinion is that you're both right."

She began to back towards the door, watching them intently, just in case they decided to switch their anger from each other to her.

As she reached the batwing doors and eased through them the thought occurred to her that this was not really the best way to keep her promise to the sheriff about staying out of trouble, but it had definitely been a way to boost her sagging wallet!

CHAPTER SEVEN

She became aware of someone's presence at her window almost immediately.

She had returned to her room earlier with her winnings and had gone directly to bed, hanging her gunbelt on the bedpost above her head. Now, as she heard the creaking of the roof outside her window and the sound of the window itself being opened, she reached for the gun with her back to the action, relying solely on her ears to tell her when the right time would be to turn around.

Whoever it was, was not particularly light of foot. As he lifted his foot over the sill to enter she heard the toe of a boot strike the wood, and a whispered curse. Her ears told her that one foot was in the room, and as she waited for the other she heard, instead, the sound of a gun being cocked.

Springing into action she rolled off the bed away from the window, taking her gun with her, and hitting the floor with a loud thump.

"Hey, what —" the intruder said, followed by a flash of light as he fired his gun.

On the floor she scrambled to the foot of the bed, raised herself up and fired at the figure silhouetted against the moonlight coming in the window. Her shot was true, striking the man in the torso as he straddled the window sill, one foot in and one foot out. He grunted, dropped his gun, slid out the window and tumbled down the graded rooftop until he fell off the end to the street below.

The two shots had attracted attention immediately. She could hear footsteps in the hall as people were trying to locate the source. She walked to the lamp on the wall by the door and turned up the light, listening to the commotion in the hall.

"What was that. . . ."

"A shot. . . ."

"Where'd it come from. . . ."

"Jesus, what's going on. . . ."

"Where's the sheriff. . . ."

"Quiet out there. I'm trying to get some sleep. . . ."

So was I, she thought as she walked to the window. From her vantage point she could see a crowd in the street but she could not see the man she had shot. Somebody lifted his head as she was looking out, saw her, and pointed, and she knew it wouldn't be long before she'd have company.

She got dressed so she'd be ready for it.

When the pounding started on the door she answered immediately, startling the sheriff, who had his fist raised to strike the door again.

"What the hell is going on?"

"Good question," she said, backing away so that he could enter.

"Didn't I tell you —" he began , then turned to the crowd in the hall and said, "Why don't you people go back to bed." He slammed the door in their faces and turned to face her again.

"Didn't I tell you to stay out of trouble?"

"Sheriff, I was sleeping in my bed. That has rarely caused trouble in the past. That man climbed through my window and took a shot at me. Would you have preferred that I didn't fire back to protect myself?"

The sheriff scowled and moved to the window to look out.

"Just move the damn body and break it up!" he shouted. "This ain't a show."

He turned to face her and she asked him, "Who was he?"

"Stranger in town, came in with three other men. I saw them playing poker at Metzger's earlier."

"Oh."

He frowned and said, "What's that mean?"

"Well . . . I was playing poker at Metzger's earlier tonight."

"With those four?"

She nodded.

"They were trying to cheat me and I sort of turned the tables on them."

"You cheated them?"

"They were so clumsy about it I couldn't resist."

"How much did you take off of them?"

"Over five hundred."

"Jesus Christ, woman! It isn't bad enough you had to go into a saloon after dark, but you had to show up four men playing poker? Is that what you call staying out of trouble? Is that the best you can do?"

"They asked me to play, Sheriff. How was I supposed to know they wanted to cheat me?"

"Women don't play poker with men."

"Is that a fact? I find that attitude a little outdated, Sheriff."

"I'm not going to argue men and women's places in this world with you," he said. "Let's just talk about your place and my place in this town."

He moved towards her and showed her his index finger. She had a good view of it because it was about an inch from the tip of her nose.

"I am the sheriff and you are a stranger drifting through my town. I make the rules and you obey them. Is that clear?"

"Very," she said, clenching her teeth to bite back a sharp retort.

"I take a very dim view of killings in my town."

"How about the fact that he fired first?"

"After you took their money didn't it ever occur to you that one of them might try to take it back?"

"To tell you the truth . . . no!"

"Then you got a lot to learn, lady. I've got a good mind to make you walk out of town."

"But you won't."

He glared at her for a few seconds, then said, "No, I won't." He turned and walked towards the door. "It's obvious that your story is true, and that he was climbing through your window to either rob you or kill you."

"I appreciate your faith."

"But I'm telling you this," he said, "If there's one more incident, you're gone from my town, even if you have to fly out!"

He slammed the door on his way out and she went to her window and closed it. She propped her boots on the window sill so that no one could open the window without knocking them to the floor. Rather than dress for bed again she simply turned down the lamp and reclined on the bed fully dressed.

After all, there were still three more men out there who wanted their money.

CHAPTER EIGHT

Clay Hammet woke up in a cell. His head was pounding and his mouth felt as if it were filled with sand from a desert. For a moment he was unsure of his surroundings. He sat up on the cot he'd been sleeping on, looked around, and then got quickly to his feet. It was then that he noticed his gun and gunbelt were missing.

"Hey!" he shouted, but his head hurt too much to continue.

"You awake?" Sheriff Toliver asked.

Hammet looked at the sheriff, who was standing at the door of the cell holding a mug in his hand. Steam rose from it, as did the aroma of coffee.

"What the hell happened?" he demanded.

"You had a little too much to drink last night, Clay, my boy."

"And you put me in here? What'd I bust up?"

"Nothing."

"I owe somebody money?"

"Nope."

Hammet lurched toward the closed cell door and said, "Then why —" but as his hands touched the door it swung open.

"You just needed a place to sleep it off, and I needed you someplace where I could keep an eye on you. Here," the sheriff said, offering him the coffee, "this is for you."

Hammet took the hot mug and sipped some of the strong, black brew. Toliver turned and walked into his office, and Hammet followed.

"Where's my gun?"

"In a safe place."

"I want it."

"And I'll give it to you, but first sit down and finish your coffee."

Grudgingly — because if he didn't sit he might fall — Hammet sat across the desk from the sheriff.

"You gonna give me another lecture?"

"I sure am. I'm trying to save your life, boy."

"I can take Angel Eyes, Toliver, and you know it."

"No, I don't know it, but even if you can, somewhere down the road there's a man with a gun who can take you. That's the one I'm trying to save you from."

"Bull. Ain't nobody can take me with a gun."

"That's what they said about Hickok."

"He wasn't killed fair."

"What's fair got to do with it, boy? You better get that kind of thinking out of your head. A smart man never kills fair, he kills dead!"

"Then he ain't a man."

"But he's alive, damn it! That's what counts."

"Jack McCall ain't alive."

"No, he ain't. He killed Hickok and he paid for it, but there's lots of other back-shooters out there, Clay. Why set yourself up as a target for one of them?"

"Because it's all I can do," Hammet said, putting the empty coffee mug on the end of the sheriff's desk. "Can I have my gun now?"

"You can have it, but let me tell you something." Toliver took the gunbelt out of his desk drawer and put it on top of the desk. "If you use this gun within the town limits, I'll come after you, Clay. You'll have to face me with a gun."

Hammet stood up and strapped on his gun.

"You wouldn't go up against me with a gun, Sheriff."

"Don't try me, Clay. You'll lose."

"You're just a town sheriff," Hammet said arrogantly. "If you was anything else you wouldn't be here. I don't want to end up like you, Toliver, upholding the law in a one-horse town when I'm fifty years old."

"No, you'll be dead way before you're fifty years old."

"But at least I'll have lived my life, and not wasted it."

"Clay, I hope the day you take a bullet, whether it's in front or in back, you'll think back to this conversation."

"I'll forget about this as soon as I go out that door."

And as Hammet did go out the door Toliver said, "That's what I'm afraid of."

Liz woke up and looked at her boots on the window. She used the basin and water on the dresser to clean up, then took the boots off the window and put them on. Strapping on her gun she left in search of breakfast.

She went to Louise's Cafe and ordered ham and eggs and biscuits from the woman. When Louise brought them, with a pot of coffee, the woman sat down at the table with her.

"Heard you had some excitement last night."

"Good news travels fast."

"What's it like to kill a man?"

"It's not fun, Louise."

"I'll bet it's exciting."

"No."

Louise looked disappointed.

"I've thought about it you know," she said, then.

"What?"

"Killing someone. I've thought about it."

"Everybody thinks about it; the trick is not to do it."

"I guess so." She looked past Liz to the door and said, "Another customer."

"Don't mind me."

The woman stood up and walked away, and Liz began to rush through her breakfast. She decided not to eat there anymore. It would be bad for her digestion.

"Angel Eyes," a voice said at her shoulder.

She turned her head very slowly and looked up into the face of Clay Hammet.

"Hello Hammet," she said. "Sit down and have some breakfast."

"Not with you."

"Why not?"

"Because I'm gonna kill you."

"Before or after breakfast?"

"Don't get smart with me."

"Who me? Smart? If I was, you think I'd be here?"

"I'm gonna kill you," he said again.

"You've got a one-track mind, kid," she said. Hammet was a "kid" to her, even though they were close in age. "Did Sheriff Toliver talk to you about this at all?"

"You can't hide behind him."

"He talked to you, then."

"Yeah, he told me to forget about it."

"That's good advice."

"Not for me."

"Look," Liz said, putting her fork down. "If you're not going to kill me now I'd really like to finish my breakfast in peace. Is that okay with you?"

"Yeah, that's fine," he said. "I'm gonna have some breakfast myself, but sooner or later you're gonna have to face me. You won't know when or where, but you will."

"If you're trying to make me sweat, kid," she said, "try harder."

"You'll see," Hammet said, "you'll see."

He walked to the other end of the small cafe and took a table. He gave Louise his order, but his eyes never left Liz.

She definitely wasn't coming here anymore.

CHAPTER NINE

After breakfast Liz went to the undertaker's office to see the man she had killed.

"I guess it's all right, seein' as how you was the one who killed him," the undertaker said. He was a man in his fifties with a long, angular face and huge, sad eyes. "I got to warn you, he ain't got no clothes on."

"I've seen naked men before."

That brought a cackle of delight from the man, but at least he had the good sense not to make a comment.

Liz followed him into his back room where he had the dead man laid out on a table.

"That's him."

Her bullet had caught him right beneath the breast bone, and his head looked to be lying at an odd angle.

"Broke his neck when he fell off the roof," the undertaker explained. "One or t'other killed him, your bullet or the fall. Don't really matter which, does it?''

"No, it doesn't.''

She looked at his face and recognized him as either Lee or Ben, one of the brothers she had played poker with the night before. That was all she needed now, a revenge seeking brother on her trail as well as a trigger happy kid.

"Seen enough?''

"More than enough. What was his name?''

"Ben Sherman.''

"Has his brother been in today?''

The man nodded.

"Him and some friends, to make the arrangements. They're comin' after you.''

"Did they say that?''

"They did.''

"To you?''

He shook his head.

"To each other, but I heard. They're coming after you, all right.''

"That's just fine.''

She left the undertaker's and walked to the livery to check on Blossom's progress.

"She's in fine shape,'' Jed said, "but that hoof is still tender. I'd give her another couple of days yet before I rode her — that is, unless you want to ruin her.''

"No danger of that,'' Liz said, giving the mare an affectionate pat. "You rest up, girl. I'll do whatever I have to do to see that you get enough rest.''

"Hear you had some excitement last night.''

"Good news travels fast."

"I could maybe sell you a horse. You could leave town. I'll give you a good price for her."

"Not a chance."

"I could loan you a horse and you could walk her out."

"Why would you do that?"

"Wouldn't want to end up with her just because you got killed. I figure you're better off leaving."

"If I left I'd have to travel slow. They'd catch up with me easy."

"That's true."

"I'll stay around awhile, Jed. Thanks for taking care of her."

"My pleasure, ma'am."

She left the livery and headed back to her hotel. The best place for her was her room, although she hated the thought of locking herself away.

As she approached her hotel she looked across the street and saw Clay Hammet sitting in a chair, watching her. She did not acknowledge his presence.

Look at that bitch, Hammet thought, as he watched Liz Archer walk toward her hotel. Damn she was beautiful, but he couldn't let that stop him. He had a reputation to make. Besides, she was a stuck-up bitch and would probably have considered herself too good for him.

He was gonna visit Dolly again tonight as soon as it got dark, but while he was fucking her he was going to be thinking of Liz Archer.

Stuck-up bitch!

There were four other men in town who were thinking about Liz Archer at that same moment.

In Clearwater's other hotel Jake, Bull and Lee were sitting in a hotel room, discussing how they were going to kill Liz Archer.

"First she takes our money, and then she kills Ben. We're not gonna let her get away with that, are we Jake?" Bull asked.

"No Bull, we're not," Jake said. He looked at Lee and said, "We'll get the bitch for killing your brother, Lee, I swear it."

"If you say so, Jake."

Jesus, Jake thought, he's almost as dumb as his idiot brother was. What the hell could Ben have been thinking of, climbing in that woman's window like that? What ever possessed him to act on his own like that? He'd never shown any sign of being able to think for himself before, so why now? Unless he hadn't been thinking for himself. What if someone else put the idea in his head? Like Lee — no, not Lee. He was even dumber than Ben. What about Bull? But why would he send Ben after the woman?

"Sure," Jake said, "I say so, Lee."

"How are we gonna do it?" Bull asked.

"I'll figure that out, Bull," Jake said. "Don't you worry. I'll figure that out."

In his office Sheriff Al Toliver was also thinking about Liz Archer. Liz Archer had been known to make a lot of men think the thoughts Al Toliver was thinking just then.

But Toliver was not used to such thoughts. Oh, he

thought about women all right, and went to Zelda's every time the need arose. He also knew that Louise McQuinn — a fine figure of a woman — had eyes for him. Not that McQuinn had anything to worry about. Toliver would never take a friend's wife to bed.

Liz Archer was different though. For one thing she was about half his age and even when he went to Zelda's he picked out the older women so he wouldn't feel like he was robbing the cradle. Still, as young as she was there was a maturity about her, which may have stemmed from the kind of life she'd been leading. One thing being on the prod as a young man had done for Al Toliver had been to age him fast, and the same thing could probably be said for the woman known as Angel Eyes.

He wanted Angel Eyes to leave town in order to avoid any more trouble, whether it be with Clay or with the dead man's brother and friends, but he also wanted her to stay, and it had been a long time since Al Toliver had been of two such separate minds.

He took his feet down from the desk, acutely aware of the erection that was raging inside his pants. He had to make his rounds, but later on he was going to have to go to Zelda's to get the condition taken care of.

CHAPTER TEN

Toliver made his morning rounds and in the course of them saw Clay Hammet sitting across the street from Liz Archer's hotel. He considered approaching the young man and then decided against it. There was a more immediate concern.

He went to the other Clearwater Hotel — which simply had a sign outside proclaiming "Hotel" — and asked the desk clerk what room the three strangers were in.

"There were four, Sheriff," the man said.

"One of them got himself killed last night, Arn. I want to talk to the other three. Are they up there?"

"Far as I know they are."

"Fine."

Toliver mounted the steps to the second floor, experiencing no apprehension whatsoever at the thought of facing three men alone. Hell, he had no choice in the matter since he had no deputies, so what was the use of worrying about it?

He knocked on the door of the three men's room, and it was opened immediately as if they were on their way out.

"Sheriff," one of them said, standing in the doorway. "We was just on our way out to get some breakfast."

"It can wait," Toliver said. He put his hand against the man's chest and shoved him out of the doorway. The man staggered back a few feet, struck the bed with the back of his knees and sat down. The other two men in the room stared.

"You got no call to do that," the man seated on the bed said.

Actually, it was the only way Toliver knew to treat hardcases like this. If someone had treated him like that earlier in his life, he might have straightened out a lot sooner.

"Just shut up and listen. You three can have your breakfast and then I want you on your horses and out of Clearwater."

"We got our friend's funeral —"

"Just plant him and get!" Toliver snapped. "He was dumb enough to get himself killed; the rest of you better be smart enough to leave it alone."

"You mean you think we're gonna go after the bitch —" the man on the bed started, but Toliver had come here to do all the talking and none of the listening.

He took a step forward and backhanded the man across the face. The burly man took one step toward him, but Toliver held a hand out as a warning.

"Take another step, friend, and I'll break you off at the knees."

The man stopped, unsure of himself.

"I'm telling you three for the only time, not the last time mind you, but for the *only* time. Bury your dead and get out of town!"

Toliver backed towards the door, which had never been shut after he'd entered. The man on the bed glared at him, blood seeping from a cut on his bottom lip. The burly man clenched and unclenched his fists, and the third man stood with a stupid look on his face waiting for someone to tell him what to do.

"This is not advice, and it's not something that I'm going to repeat," Toliver said. "It's not a warning, either. It's fact. If I see any of you in town after today, you'll have to deal with me."

He backed into the hall and pulled the door shut, then waited a few seconds to see if anyone would follow him. He heard some movement from inside, but the door remained closed so he left.

Inside the room Jake Pringle wiped his hand across his face, smearing the back of it with blood.

"That sheriff is a dead man."

"He's tough," Lee said.

"He ain't so tough," Bull said.

"I didn't see you taking him on," Jake said.

"I didn't see you, either."

Jake opened his mouth to reply, then shut it and thought again.

"All right, let's not fight among ourselves. Let's get things in order here. First the girl goes, and then the lawman. Anybody got any objections?"

"No," Bull said.

"Whatever you say, Jake," Lee said.

"Yeah," Jake said, wiping his mouth again, "whatever I say."

Leaving the hotel Al Toliver made a decision. Since Clay Hammet wanted to be a hardcase, like those three upstairs, then maybe Toliver should start treating him like one — and there was only one way to treat a hardcase!

Liz's room overlooked the street, and she could see Hammet still sitting in a chair across the street. She felt closed in, not because she was afraid of him or of the three poker players, but because she'd promised the sheriff to stay out of trouble. There had to be a way of doing that though, without staying cooped up in her room like a disobedient child.

As she stared out the window she saw the sheriff striding purposefully towards Clay Hammet, who was now reclining with his feet up, his chair leaning back on the rear two legs with the front two in the air.

Toliver stopped next to him, said something, and then kicked the chair out from under him.

"I said get up!" Toliver snapped again, looking down at the fallen Hammet.

"What the hell's the matter with you?" Hammet demanded, climbing to his feet and righting his chair. "I was just sitting —"

"You were loitering," Toliver said, "and if I see you loitering again I'll lock your ass up!"

Hammet stared at Toliver with his mouth open for a few seconds, and then a knowing look came over his face as he thought he understood.

"I get it. You're taking her side."

"Wrong. I'm taking my side, and you better remember that," Toliver said, prodding the boy hard in the chest with his forefinger.

"Don't do that to me."

"Why not?" Toliver asked, repeating the move.

"Don't push me, Sheriff."

"Why not, Clay?" Toliver asked, this time pushing the younger man with the flat palm of his hand. "You're pushing me, aren't you?"

"I ain't —"

"You're planning gunplay in my town, aren't you?" Toliver asked, pushing him again. "That's pushing me."

"I'm warning you —"

"I do the warning in Clearwater, Clay," Toliver said, cutting him off. "Remember that."

He pushed Hammet again, almost knocking him completely off balance, and he saw the man lose control. Hammet swung at him and Toliver blocked the punch easily and hit the younger man in the stomach. He fell to the boardwalk in a seated position, rocking back and forth and fighting for his breath.

Toliver crouched down next to him so he'd be sure to hear him.

"You're out of your league, Clay, and I'm just a small-town sheriff."

Hammet looked at him, red-faced and breathless, and forced out a reply between clenched teeth.

"You . . . ain't . . . savin' . . . her. . . ."

"You idiot," Toliver said wearily, standing up. "I'm trying to save you, not her."

"Fuck . . . you. . . ."

"Clay," Toliver said shaking his head. "If you're gonna play hardcase in my town I'm going to have to treat you just like the others."

"You'll . . . be . . . sorry. . . ."

I already am, Toliver thought.

He looked up at the hotel then and saw Liz Archer standing in her window. He decided that since he was making the rounds of troublemakers he might as well go and talk to her as well. He left Hammet there on the ground and crossed the street toward the hotel.

CHAPTER ELEVEN

Liz was waiting for the knock on the door and opened it immediately.

"Did you come here to beat me up, too?"

"You watched."

"I did. What were you trying to prove?"

"I couldn't get through to him one way, so I thought I'd try another."

"Think it worked?"

He scowled and said, "No."

"Too bad."

"I talked to the dead man's friends, too. Told them to get out of town."

"Think they'll listen?"

"They'd better."

"And now you came up here to talk to me."

"Yes," he said, but the look in his eyes — which

she was seeing there for the first time — said he wanted to do more than talk.

"Sheriff."

"Yeah."

"You going to talk?"

He rubbed his jaw, staring at her. She was the prettiest thing he'd ever seen — no, the most beautiful thing. But he was an old man, almost fifty-one. Would she? . . .

"Sheriff."

"What?"

"Close the door."

"What?" he asked, in a different tone of voice.

"If we're going to . . . talk, I think we'd be more comfortable with the door closed don't you?"

Was she saying what he thought she was saying.

"Damn it, lawdog, shut the door and kiss me!"

"By God!" he said, slamming the door behind him and striding towards her.

They did considerably more than kiss.

He undressed her, his hands fumbling at her buttons, and then she undressed him. She took his raging penis into her mouth then and he grabbed her head while she sucked him, amazed that it was even happening.

Later they moved to the bed and he mounted her, piercing her easily, pounding away at her furiously while she closed her legs and thighs around him and raked her nails across his back.

"Damn," he said later, "I'm too old for this."

They were lying in bed and he was fighting to catch his breath.

"No you're not," she said, winding his gray chest hairs around her fingers.

"I didn't plan this, you know. I mean, when I came up here —"

"I know," she assured him. "You came up here to beat me up."

"I didn't —" he began to protest, but she cut him off with a laugh and a kiss.

"You're so serious."

"This is a serious situation."

"This one?" she asked, prodding his belly with her fingernail.

"Not this right here," he said, "but the whole thing. Clay Hammet, the three strangers. I shouldn't be up here with you like this. You're so damned young."

"Is that against the law?" she asked.

"No."

"Should I be up here with Clay Hammet instead, just because he's closer to my age?"

"I guess not."

"You're not sorry, are you?"

"Hell, no."

"Are you ready again?"

"Jesus, no . . ." he said, but she decided that he was.

And she was right.

Clay Hammet was across the street, sitting in the chair and holding his sore belly. He was glaring at the hotel, waiting for Toliver to come out, and then it hit him.

"He's fucking her," he said aloud. "The old coot is fucking her!"

No wonder he was taking her side. She was using

her pussy to get the law on her side and Toliver, the old fool, was going for it.

He decided he needed a drink and stood up. Walking to the saloon he figured this changed things. There was no way he'd get a fair shake in this town now, so he was going to have to make some plans.

"Where'd you learn how to use a gun?" Toliver asked later.

"Are you going to answer questions about your past?"

"No."

"Then I won't about mine."

He turned his head to look at her and said, "Maybe later, when we know each other better."

She snaked her hand beneath the covers to cup his balls and said, "Could we know each other better?"

"We could," he said, "but not today."

She smiled and closed her hand over him.

"Want to bet?" she asked, just before she crawled under the covers.

"This might work to our advantage," Al Toliver said as he got dressed.

"How?" Liz asked, watching him. For a man his age he was in excellent condition. He was thick and hard and, though he certainly looked his age, there was a youthful vitality in him that appealed to her.

"Come with me and have lunch."

"Why?"

"If we're seen together maybe it will warn Clay off."

She frowned and asked, "You want him to know that we're . . . friends?"

"You don't think it will work?"

"Al, you've known him a long time."

"Yes."

"Are you friends?"

"We're too far apart for that."

"Still, if he sees us together he might feel as if you betrayed him."

Toliver stopped and said, "I didn't think of that. You're pretty smart, aren't you?"

"If I was smart," she asked, "would I have stopped off in a town called Clearwater?" She shivered then, pulled the sheet and blanket up over her and added, "A *cold* town called Clearwater?"

"I'm glad you did," he said, and then added, "I think."

"Al, I'll try and stay out of trouble, really I will, but I don't think I can stay cooped up here."

"Not even if I bring you your meals?"

"Like a prisoner?"

He strapped on his gun and looked down at her.

"I guess not. Look, come with me and have lunch. If he's going to feel betrayed he does by now. I've been in here a while and he can probably guess what's been going on."

"All right," she said. She flipped back the covers and put her feet on the cold floor. Immediately, her body sprouted goose pimples and she shouted, "My clothes, get me my clothes!" He took his own sweet time handing them to her.

CHAPTER TWELVE

They had lunch at a cafe down the street, but not Louise's Cafe.

"I don't think we should go in there," Liz had said. "We've got enough trouble with the other people who want to kill me. I don't want to add her to the list."

Now, over lunch, he asked her a question he had asked earlier.

"How'd you get so good with a gun?"

"I thought we said —"

"How much longer will you be here for us to get to know each other better?" he asked.

"Does that mean you'll talk, too?"

"Yes."

"All right," she said, and told him the story of how her family and fiancé were killed, how she'd took out after them and met a man who taught her to use a gun.

When her story was finished he said, "Who was the man?"

"A travelling gunsmith I thought at the time, but I later found out he was much, much more."

"Well, who was he?"

"His name is Tate Gilmore."

"Gilmore!"

"You've heard of him, I see."

Instead of answering Toliver began to laugh and she looked on, puzzled.

"What's so funny?" she asked after the laughter had died down.

"Nothing, it's just that Tate Gilmore and I go back a ways, that's all."

"You knew Tate?"

"A long time ago, when we were both making our way with our guns."

"You?"

"Is that so hard to believe?"

"Well, no. . . ."

"Sure it is. Well, when I was younger I thought I was as fast as God, just like Clay Hammet does, only I learned quickly that fast doesn't mean you'll always come out on top."

"How fast were you?"

"Not as fast as Tate," he said, shaking his head. "That man could make a gun appear in his hand like magic. I don't think I ever knew a man as fast, and I knew plenty. Hickok, Clay Allison, Ben Thompson, Earp, Masterson. I've seen or known them all."

"And Tate's the best?"

"He had it all, Liz. He wasn't just fast, he was calm, he was accurate — hell, he still is, for all I know. When did you see him last?"

"Last year," she said, and then with a wistful note she added, "I haven't seen him since."

Toliver stared at her and then said, "You're in love with him, aren't you?"

"I thought I loved a man once," she said, "but I was wrong. Now I guess if I could ever love a man it would be Tate Gilmore."

"He always was a lucky dog. Luck was something else he had on his side. He's younger than me, but I guess I was always in awe of him. Jesus, I haven't seen Tate in over ten years."

Having found common ground they talked about Tate Gilmore for awhile, as Toliver felt no jealousy toward Tate.

Later, Liz turned the conversation back to Toliver's life.

"So you've been sheriff of this town for a long time?" she asked.

"About eight years, I guess. I wore a badge a few other places, but finally decided to settle down here."

"Why?"

"It's quiet and peaceful most of the time, and I can count on the fingers of one hand the times I've actually had to use my gun."

"I hope you won't have to use it for a long time to come."

Reminded of the present situation, he frowned and said, "Let's hope not."

"I wonder if those three have left town yet."

"We can check at the undertaker's and see if they buried their dead friend. Have you finished your lunch?"

"I've had enough."

"Let's do that, then. The quicker they've gone, the quicker we can concentrate on the problem of Clay Hammet."

CHAPTER THIRTEEN

They went to the undertaker's office and found that the three had already picked up their dead.

"I asked them if they wanted me to bury him, but they said they'd do it themselves. Seemed in an awful hurry they did, Sheriff."

"Thanks, Elias."

"Sure," he said, giving Toliver and Liz the eye. "Anything else I can do for you?"

"No, nothing. Thanks."

They walked outside and Liz asked, "What do you think? Are they gone?"

"Maybe," he said. "Let's check the livery."

At the livery they got the same story from Jed.

"They took all four of their horses, Sheriff. Said they was gonna toss their friend over his and take him out of town that way. They said they was in a hurry to leave town."

"Uh-huh."

"Your mare's doing fine, miss."

"Thank you, Jed."

Outside Liz said, "Well?"

"One more place."

They checked with Arnie, the clerk at the hotel where the men had been staying, and got the same story.

"They was in an awful hurry to leave, Sheriff," Arnie said. "They said so."

"Thanks, Arn."

On the street Liz said, "What's bothering you, Al?"

"They made damn sure they told enough people that they were in a hurry to leave town."

"Which makes you think they haven't?"

"No, they've left town all right," Toliver said, "I'm just wondering how long it's going to take them to come back."

They went to Toliver's office, where he made them some strong coffee.

"You figure them to bury the dead man and then double back," she said.

"I do."

"You don't think you scared them off?"

He sighed.

"Those tactics don't work real good anymore, Liz. They used to, but not anymore. More often than not you get the fella real mad at you instead of scaring him."

"Why use them then?"

"Because I'm an old dog and I'm not learning any new tricks these days."

"If they come back, are they coming for you, or for me?" she asked.

"My guess would be you first, and then me."

"You have any deputies?"

"No."

"Could you get any?"

"I've been handling the law in this town for a long time, Liz. I don't think any of the townspeople are prepared to start helping me."

"What about me?"

"You want to be a deputy?"

"You got any better ideas?"

"Why don't we just make it unofficial, between you and me."

"You worried about Hammet?"

He nodded.

"If I put a badge on you he's bound to think I'm trying to hide you behind it."

"I've got another idea, then."

"What?"

"Offer a badge to him."

"And give him official status when he tries to kill you?" Toliver asked.

"Maybe not; maybe he'll take the badge serious."

"He wouldn't take it at all. He'd rather die than become a small-town lawman."

"He said so?"

"On many occasions. He doesn't want to end up like me, he says."

"He could do a lot worse."

Toliver smiled and said, "Maybe you and I know that, but he doesn't."

"Well, maybe you could recruit him unofficially."

"You forget, I treated him just the way I treated the other three. I think they'd have a better chance of getting him on their side."

"Then it's just you and me."

"Looking over our shoulders."

"What happens if Blossom is ready to leave tomorrow?" she asked.

"Then you leave. At least that would take care of the situation with Hammet."

"And that would leave you to face those other three alone."

"Unless they take off after you," he reasoned, rubbing his jaw. "Which means you'd be the one who'd have to face them alone."

"I'd be willing to take that chance."

"So would I."

They stared at each other until Liz broke the silence.

"So we're both going to be stubborn."

"Looks that way."

"In that case," she said, "do you have any more of this terrible coffee?"

He smiled and said, "All you want."

CHAPTER FOURTEEN

Outside of town Jake Pringle was camped with Bull Benton and Lee Sherman.

"When are we going in, Jake?" Lee asked.

"When I say so, Lee," Jake said impatiently. "Now just keep quiet and go look after the horses."

"Sure, Jake."

When Lee was gone Jake said to Bull, "Look, I've got an idea."

"What?"

"If we're going to do this why don't we go all the way?"

"What do you mean?"

Jake leaned forward, elbows on his knees and said, "If we're going to kill the lawman, why don't we rob the bank while we're at it?"

"That's big time, Jake," Bull said. "All we've ever done is con some people."

"Yeah, with that poker dodge," Jake said. "Small change, Bull. That bitch was right about one thing, I'm a second-rater at dealing seconds. I'm tired of being a second-rater, Bull, and the money in that bank is gonna make me first-rate. It'll make *us* first-rate."

"You mean the three of us?"

"I mean," Jake said, looking over to where Lee was standing with the horses, "the two of us."

"I don't know, Jake," Bull said, scratching his neck. "We're not bank robbers."

"What is there to it? We go in with our guns and hold up the bank. We leave Lee outside with the horses."

"We'll be chased by a posse."

"The whole time we were in that town did you ever see a deputy?"

Bull thought about it and then said, "No, but —"

"Once we get rid of the sheriff there won't be anybody to round up a posse. Besides," Jake said, looking at Lee again, "we'll leave them something to satisfy them for awhile. What do you say, Bull?"

"What about the girl? We gonna bother with the five hundred she took from us?"

"Sure we are. Every little bit will help, and I ain't about to let no little gal get the best of Jake Pringle. Are you with me, Bull?"

Bull looked over at Lee and then said, "I'm with you, Jake."

"Okay," Jake said, "here's how I want to lay it out. . . ."

Clay Hammet was standing at the bar in Metzger's

drinking whiskey and eating hardboiled eggs from a bowl that was sitting on top of the bar.

"What's your problem?" the bartender asked. "I thought you was as happy as a pig in shit."

"I was, but the sheriff has decided to turn traitor."

"What does that mean?"

"He's siding against me."

"With the girl, you mean?"

"That's right."

"Why would he do that?"

"Because he likes that fur pelt between her legs, that's why."

The bartender looked surprised and said, "Al Toliver and Angel Eyes?"

"That's right."

"I can't believe it —"

Hammet grabbed the front of the bartender's shirt and said, "You calling me a liar?"

"Take it easy, Clay," the man said, grabbing Hammet's wrists. "Nobody's calling you a liar. I just said it was hard to believe. Toliver's no youngster, you know? How old is this Angel Eyes gal?"

Hammet let go of the man's shirt and said, "I don't know, a little older than me, I guess."

"Jesus."

"Yeah. Siding against one of his own."

"Maybe he's just going according to the law."

"By fucking her? Is that the law? The gal spreads her legs and is in the right?"

"I guess not."

"You're damn right! I live in this town, damn it, and she's just a stranger."

"Yeah, but she didn't come here aiming to kill anyone," the bartender pointed out.

"I don't care."

"Well, what are you gonna do, Clay?"

"I ain't gonna let it stop me, that's for sure," Hammet said, taking the last egg from the bowl. "Got any more of these eggs, Ed?"

"Why don't you have some dinner, Clay —"

"The eggs are free, ain't they?"

"As long as you put salt on them."

Hammet picked up the salt shaker and shook some onto the egg, then popped it into his mouth.

"Got more eggs?"

"Coming up."

"And a beer, too."

"What about the whiskey?"

Hammet looked at the bottle in front of him, about three quarters full, and said, "Take it back. If I'm gonna figure this out I got to be sober. Just bring me a beer because I got a powerful thirst."

The bartender shook his head and went for more eggs. How the hell could a kid who couldn't figure out that the salt on the eggs was making him thirsty figure anything else out?

CHAPTER FIFTEEN

The way Jake had it figured, the only man who would respond to the bank robbery was the sheriff, since he had no deputies. From there it would be fairly easy to gun him down. As for the woman he'd decided that she would be killed only if it fit into their plan. Once they robbed the bank they couldn't very well go looking for her, and if they went looking for her first they might be spotted before they robbed the bank.

"If we can't get her, the five hundred will have to be taken as a loss."

"What about letting her get away with what she did?" Bull asked.

Jake shrugged and said, "A lot of money can take care of that, Bull."

Bull had to agree with that.

"Besides, we might run into her again someplace else. Who knows?"

So it was agreed.

The morning that the "gang" was going to rob the bank Liz and Toliver woke in different beds. Toliver was too old to think that one afternoon in bed together made them lovers, and Liz was simply letting the sheriff take the lead this time. If he wanted her again, he would let her know.

So they slept apart, which thoroughly confused Clay Hammet. Standing outside her hotel he expected to see the sheriff sooner or later, but late the previous night he'd given up and gone to Zelda's. After a satisfying night with Dolly he returned to his position across from the hotel. He wouldn't have been surprised to see the sheriff come out, but he didn't. In fact, he saw the lawman come out of his office — where he also slept — and sank back into a doorway to avoid being seen.

It would have to be today, he decided. As soon as the bitch came out of the hotel he'd brace her and force her to draw. When it was over, he'd be a big man in this town and the sheriff wouldn't dare try anything.

The gang rode into town early, just as the bank opened. The streets were not yet alive. They left Lee outside with the horses and Jake and Bull went inside, drew their guns, and announced a stick-up.

Toliver was in the cafe being served breakfast by a very attentive Louise when someone burst in with the news.

"The bank's being robbed!"

He stood up and ran out of the cafe towards the bank.

As Liz Archer exited from the hotel Clay Hammet stepped forward into the street. She spotted him and stopped cold.

"Angel Eyes!"

"Don't do this, Clay," she said.

"I'm gonna prove it to you, this town and to Toliver. I'm the fastest gun there is."

"Clay, this is wrong. There's no need for one of us to die."

"Hah! You're scared."

"I'm afraid, all right — afraid that I'll have to kill you."

Peripherally she became aware of some commotion in another part of town, but she dared not take her eyes off of Hammet.

Toliver rushed towards the bank just as the two men came running out, each carrying a canvas sack. He recognized them immediately.

"Hold it!"

Jake turned and fired. On the sidelines a woman lost her grasp on her child, a seven-year-old girl, who chose that moment to dash across the street. She was thinking of peppermint sticks in a jar, and not of the danger of flying bullets.

Toliver, about to draw his gun, saw the little girl and went for her instead. He grabbed her up and turned his back to shield her with his body. Jake's bullet punched him just over the kidney on the right side. He staggered and put the little girl down, sending her running back in her mother's direction, crying. He turned, drawing his gun, just as Jake fired again. This time the bullet caught him high on the left side in the shoulder. He was still able to draw and fire but with no accuracy at all. His shot went wild. Jake fired again, but this time his bullet punched into Lee's stomach cancelling the necessity of a three way split.

Toliver saw this as he fell putting out his uninjured arm to break his fall. His gun fell from his hand and he was helpless to stop them from riding out.

"Something's going on, Clay," Liz said as she heard the shots.

"I don't care about anything but what's happening right here."

"Clay —"

Somebody came running toward them and they both turned to look at him. It was the hotel clerk, Clem.

"The bank's been robbed and the sheriff's been shot."

He ran on to continue his news. Liz exchanged looks with Clay.

"The sheriff . . ." Clay said.

"Can we put this off until later, Clay?"

As his answer Clay started running toward the bank with Liz close on his heels.

CHAPTER SIXTEEN

By the time they reached the scene the bank robbers were gone, except the one who lay in the street. There was a group of people gathered in a circle, and she assumed that this was where Al Toliver was lying — alive or dead.

"Excuse me," she said, trying to follow the path Clay Hammet was making through the circle.

When she got to the center she saw Hammet kneeling down by Toliver. There was a man on the other side of the fallen lawman also, apparently a doctor. The sheriff looked to be alive, but he was lying in a fair amount of blood. From what she could see he'd been shot twice, and the doctor was trying to staunch the flow of blood.

"Al?" she heard Hammet say. It was the first time she'd ever heard him say the sheriff's name.

Toliver's eyes flickered open and he looked at Clay Hammet.

"Dumb kid," he said and then closed his eyes.

"Is he dead?" Hammet asked, genuine concern in his tone.

"Not yet," the doctor said, getting to his feet. "I need some men to take him to my office."

Four or five men stepped forward immediately to carry him to the doctor's office, and she wondered where they were when the bank was being robbed.

"Better have the other one moved, too," Liz said.

The doctor looked at her, then nodded and barked orders to remove the other body.

"Who can tell me what happened?" she asked. No one stepped forward and impatiently she said, "Come on, come on, somebody say something!"

Finally a woman stepped forward and when she finished telling what she had seen she added, "He saved my little girl's life. If it wasn't for her he wouldn't have gotten shot. I'm sorry!"

"You've got nothing to be sorry about," Liz told her, squeezing her arm. "Take your little girl home."

As the woman left Liz addressed the milling crowd.

"I need someone who can describe the men."

"I can," a young man said, stepping forward. He was bleeding from a scalp wound. "I'm a teller in the bank."

Liz grabbed him by the arm to steady him and asked, "Did they hurt anyone else?"

"No one."

"All right. You get over to the doctor's office and he'll look at you when he's finished with the sheriff. I'll talk to you there."

"Right."

She walked over the fallen robber as they were lifting him up and looked down at him. He was the brother of the man she'd killed trying to climb into her room. According to the woman's story he'd been shot by one of his own men.

"Guess they didn't want a three way split," she said to the dead man and headed for the doctor's office.

When Liz reached the doctor's office she found that he had chased almost everyone out. Remaining were the injured teller, holding a white cloth to his head, and Clay Hammet.

"Where is he?"

"Inside," Hammet said.

"Is he going to make it?"

Hammet shrugged, looking miserable. Liz decided that there was considerably more going on between Toliver and Hammet than either man had let on.

"Can you tell me what went on inside the bank?" she asked the teller.

"It's simple. They came in, showed their guns, and said it was a stick-up. There was only me, another clerk, and the bank manager."

"Why did they hit you?"

"I guess I wasn't moving fast enough for them."

"What about the other two men?"

"Now, that's odd," the teller said. "They kept me and the manager, but they let Randy — the other teller — go. I guess it was him who called the sheriff."

"They let him go to raise an alarm?" she asked, not sure she had heard right.

"I guess that's what they did."

"That means they wanted the sheriff to show up."

"Why?" Hammet asked.

"Because they knew he didn't have a deputy and that he'd show up late."

"Damn!"

"What?"

Hammet looked at her and said, "Last night he asked me to be his deputy."

"And?"

"I turned him down."

"I guess you must have had a good reason."

"I didn't want to end up like him."

"Well, at this point I can't blame you."

The doctor came out and they suspended their conversation.

"Doc?" Hammet asked.

Shaking his head the doctor said, "He's tough. He's got two slugs in him and he won't let go. If he can hang on through the night he'll have a good chance."

"Did you get the bullets out?" Liz asked.

"I've got to wait for him to get stronger. If he's still around tomorrow I'll go in and get them."

"That's it? That's all you can do?" Hammet asked.

"That's all any of us can do, son."

Hammet stared at the doctor, then stormed out of the office.

The doctor turned to Liz and said, "You and I seemed to be in charge out there. What are you going to do?"

"Well, since I'm Al Toliver's unofficial deputy, I guess I'll become official and go after those bank robbers."

"By tomorrow," the doctor said, "they may also be murderers."

"Yeah. . . ."

"Are you going after them alone?"

"I guess so, unless . . . unless I can get Hammet to go with me."

"Good luck trying."

"Thanks."

"Were they close?" the doctor asked Liz as she headed for the door.

"I didn't think so, up until now," she said, leaning on the doorknob.

"Funny, neither did I. I never saw two relatives who were more different —"

"Wait a minute," Liz said. "Did you say relatives?"

"Yes. Didn't you know? Toliver's sister was Clay's mother."

"The Sheriff is Clay Hammet's uncle?"

"Not so you'd notice, but yes." The doctor turned to the teller and said, "Let's have a look at you."

CHAPTER SEVENTEEN

Liz stopped off at the sheriff's office to pick something up and then found Hammet where she thought she would, in Metzger's Saloon working on a drink.

"Feeling sorry for yourself?" she asked.

"Leave me alone."

"I didn't know Al was your uncle."

"So what?"

"So what are you thinking? That if you'd signed on as a deputy this wouldn't have happened?"

"I'm thinking of my mother —" he started to say, then stopped and said, "It's none of your business what I'm thinking about."

"You're right about that. I've got something for you, from your uncle."

"Stop calling him my uncle. He was never around to be my uncle. He was always just Al."

"All right, then I've got something for you from the sheriff."

"What?"

She tossed it on the bar where it landed with a metallic sound. It was a deputy's badge, and it matched the one she was wearing on her shirt.

"What's that for?"

"You and I are deputies, and we're going after the men who robbed the bank and shot the sheriff."

"Is he? . . ."

"No, he's not dead, but I'm not waiting around for him to die. If he pulls through I want him to know that we got the men who shot him."

Hammet stared at the badge as if it would sit up and bite him at any moment.

"I'm not putting that on."

"I'm not saying you have to be a lawman from now on, Clay. Just put the damn thing on so we can start looking for the men who shot your — who shot the sheriff."

"No."

"All right, I'm going to be leaving within the hour, as soon as I can get outfitted. If you want to come, you've got that long to change your mind."

"I won't."

"I'll just leave that there while you're thinking about it."

"Take it —" he started, but she turned her back on him and walked out.

She went back to the doctor's office to see if she could speak to Toliver.

"Just for a few minutes," the doctor said, noticing the badge on her shirt.

He led her into his examining room where Toliver was lying on a table.

"I don't want him in a soft bed just yet. Don't talk too long."

"All right."

She approached the table and looked down at him. He seemed to have aged ten years.

"Al?"

He opened his eyes immediately, which she chose to see as a good sign.

"Hello, Liz."

"We're going after them, Al . . . me and Clay."

"Clay —"

"Why didn't you tell me you were his uncle?"

"Never . . . really . . . was. . . ."

"All right, forget it. I don't want you to worry about anything. Just rest and we'll be back soon with the men who shot you."

"May . . . not . . . be . . . here."

"You'll be here," she said, but he'd closed his eyes.

In the outer office she said, "Thanks, Doc. Take good care of him, will you?"

"It's in God's hands right now. If he keeps him around until tomorrow, then it'll be in mine."

Liz didn't know what to say to that so she just nodded and left.

She stopped at the General Store for some supplies, then went to the livery to see how Blossom was.

"She's fine for some easy walking, but not for riding in a posse," Jed told her.

"That's what I was afraid of. What else have you got that I can ride, Jed?"

Jed smiled then and said, "Come with me."

He took her through the livery and out back to a corral, where a huge brute stood, a dark brown gelding who easily stood sixteen hands. He had a white blaze on his face that was wide between his eyes and narrowed towards his nose, and one white sock on his right foreleg.

"Beautiful, isn't he?"

"Where did you get him?"

"Raised him up. He's three now. I'm gonna race him this season, but you can take him to track those yahoos down."

"Jed, he could be ruined for racing —"

"Al Toliver's always been good to me, Miss Liz. You take the gelding. I know you'll take care of him. He's got everything you need, stamina, speed, and smarts. You take him and find the men who shot Al."

"Could you saddle him up for me, Jed?"

"Sure."

She went back into the livery with Jed and when he went out with her saddle she waited inside. While she was waiting Clay Hammet came walking in.

He was wearing the badge.

"This doesn't change nothing between me and you, you know," he said, immediately.

"Of course not."

"When we get back we're gonna pick up right where we left off."

"Sure."

"I just don't want you to think I've changed my mind, that's all. I'm gonna be a somebody, and not just a small town lawman."

"Whatever you say Clay."

"I got to saddle my horse and get some grub."

"I got enough for both of us," she said, indicating her sack. "We'll travel light."

"You knew I'd come?"

"I didn't know," she said, "but I had a feeling you would."

"I got to saddle my horse," he said again.

As Jed led the gelding in Hammet was just tightening the cinch on his sorrel. He stopped and stared at the magnificent horse.

"Jed, that's your racing horse."

"I'm giving it to the lady, Clay, to find the men who shot Al. You going, too?"

"I am."

"I wish you both luck. Here," he said, moving into a stall and coming out with a couple of heavy blankets. "It's gonna get cold and you'll need these."

"Thanks very much, Jed," Liz said. Hammet took his without thanks.

Jed held the gelding's head while she mounted up. He tried to toss his head, but Jed held fast until Liz had the reins in her hands.

"Be firm with him."

"I will. What's his name?"

"He ain't got a name. Why don't you name him for me? If you bring him back sound I'll race him under the name you give him."

She thought a moment and then smiled and said, "I'm going to call him Tate."

"Tate it is, then."

"You ready?" she asked Hammet.

He mounted up and said, "I'm ready."

"Let's go, Tate," she said.

The horse's huge muscles bunched beneath her and for a moment she thought he was going to throw her, but then he moved forward, seeming to glide as he walked. She couldn't wait to let him run.

"I'll watch out for him, Jed."

"You get those men any way you have to, Miss Liz. I'll understand."

"You gonna talk, or ride?" Hammet asked.

"We're riding, Clay."

He spurred his horse into a canter and moved on ahead of her. She let him stay there because she felt they'd have very little to say to each other while riding side by side.

At the very best, she thought, this would be a somewhat uneasy alliance.

At the worst, it would be a disaster.

CHAPTER EIGHTEEN

A few miles out of town Clay Hammet reined his horse in and waited for Liz to catch up.

"What's wrong?" she asked.

"Nothing."

"Then why did you stop?"

He hesitated as long as he could, then said, "I don't know which way to go."

It took a moment but she finally got it.

Hammet couldn't read sign.

As a matter of fact she could barely read it herself. What little she knew she'd learned through trial and error tracking the men who killed her family, and then from the wolfer, Loren Page, whom she'd teamed up with in Montana. But what Loren had taught her applied almost exclusively to animals.

Still, if she took the same principles and applied them here, it should work.

She stared at the ground but that was no good. They were on the trail to and from town, and it had been much travelled — too much so to pick out the fresh sign. What was needed here was common sense.

"They'd stick to the trail in order to make good time early, put some daylight between them and whatever posse might follow," she said.

"They know that Toliver had no deputies. Why would they worry about a posse?"

"They'd play it safe, Clay. Let's continue on for a while. We should be able to see the point where they left the trail, or else we'll come to the trail's end. From that point on I'll read the sign."

"This doesn't mean you're in charge, you know."

"What?"

"I'm in charge."

"Why you?"

"Because I'm a man and you're a woman and that's the way it is."

"Clay, have you ever rode in a posse before? Have you ever tracked a man?"

"No, but —"

She held up her hand to silence him and said, "What do you say we just call it a partnership? We'll be equal partners with neither of us in charge."

Grudgingly, he accepted.

"But we're temporary partners."

"I wouldn't have it any other way," she said. "Let's go . . . partner."

Some distance ahead Jake Pringle held up his hand, signaling Bull to stop.

"What's the matter?"

"Nothing," Jake said, dismounting. "I want to see how much we got."

"Now? Suppose there's a posse coming?"

"Bull, I gunned that sheriff clean. You saw me. It was like fuçkin' Billy the Kid. By the time they decide who the new sheriff is and he gets up a posse we'll be long gone. Let's see what's in the bags."

Bull tossed the bag he was holding down to his partner and Jake opened both bags and began counting the money.

"Shit!"

"What's the matter?" Bull asked. He was still on his horse, looking behind them just in case a posse was coming. At the first sign of a dust cloud he wanted to be off and running.

Now he looked down at Jake and asked again, "What's the matter?"

"Eighteen hundred dollars."

"What?"

"That's all we got. One thousand eight hundred dollars and some change. Jesus!"

"That's nine hundred a piece," Bull said. "That ain't bad, Jake."

Jake put his hands on his hips and stared up at Bull Benton.

"Why are you such a small thinker, Bull? How much did you expect us to get out of that bank?"

"I never thought about it."

"Well, I did. I expected to get ten thousand dollars, at least! I would have settled for five, but what did we get?"

"One thousand —"

"I know, and eight hundred dollars. All that effort for this."

"You want to give it back?"

"Hell, no, that's not the point. I'll take it, but I don't like it."

"Uh-oh."

Now it was Jake's turn to ask, "What's the matter?"

"Dust, Jake," Bull said. "Somebody's coming after us and they're riding hard."

"Don't panic," Jake said, putting all the money in one bag and hoping that Bull wouldn't notice. He went around to his horse and mounted up.

"Maybe it's just someone coming in the same direction."

"Riding like their asses were on fire?"

"All right, let's go."

"Where's the other bag?"

Shit, Bull had noticed.

"I got it all in one bag, Bull. It's easier to carry that way. Come on, let's ride. I've got an idea, but I'll need time to tell it to you."

"You said there'd be no posse. They're gonna hang us, Jake."

"They gotta catch us first!"

Liz spotted the sign almost as soon as Hammet spotted the two men.

"I see them."

"Where?"

"They're off a ways, but you can make them out."

Hammet had good eyes. It took her a few moments,

but she finally saw them, two small stick-figures off in the distance.

"They must have been riding mighty easy for us to get this close to them," he said.

"They figured with Toliver dead there'd be no one coming after them. Come on, we'll ride easy so we won't —"

"Easy hell," Hammet said, digging his heels into his horse's side. "I'm gonna get the bastards."

"Clay, no!"

He started riding hard and immediately began kicking up dust — dust that the two men they were chasing would easily be able to see. As she started after him she could see the two men wheel their horses around and take off at a dead run.

The element of surprise was gone, and they were still too far ahead to hope to catch them. They would chase them for a while, but eventually the men would find a place to hole up and they'd lose them and have to start the search all over again.

It turned into a cat-and-mouse game that they played for the rest of the day. First they'd lose them, then they'd find them again and chase them, and then they'd lose them again. Now, as it was getting dark, Liz suggested they stop and camp.

"Are they gonna stop and camp?" Hammet asked.

"Not if they're smart."

"Then why are we —"

"Clay, they might make up some time on us in the dark, but it's not going to be that much. Trying to follow them in the dark one of our horses could step in a hole and then where would we be? No, I'd rather wait until daylight when we can travel at normal speed."

"I'd rather go on now."

"All right," she said, "this is a partnership, right? One can't tell the other what to do, right? So you go on ahead and I'll catch up when it's daylight."

She dismounted and removed the bag with their stores in it.

"I'll give you some beef jerky, if you want."

"I don't want beef jerky."

"Well you can't have coffee if you're on the move, can you?"

She was giving him an out. It was cold and coffee would go a long way toward warming them up, but she also knew — and he did, too — that if he went ahead without her there was a good chance that he would get lost.

"What's it going to be," she asked, "the cold or the coffee?"

He stared down at her for a few moments, then sighed and said, "The coffee."

"Good choice, partner."

"It's dark," Bull Benton complained, as if Jake hadn't noticed. "Ain't we gonna stop?"

"Hell, no. You think they're gonna stop? They want us so bad they're just gonna keep coming."

"That's because you shot their sheriff."

"And we all decided we were gonna do that, Bull. Remember? I just happen to be the one who pulled the trigger. It could just as well have been you or Lee."

"Sure. Good old Lee voted yes, too, didn't he? All because the sheriff backhanded you."

Jake turned in his saddle and said, "There's no point in going over all of this, Bull. What's done is done. If there had been ten thousand dollars in that bank you wouldn't be complaining, would you?"

"I suppose not," Bull had to admit.

"Let's go a little farther and I'll tell you my idea."

CHAPTER NINETEEN

They sat huddled next to the fire with blankets
around them and cups of hot coffee in their hands.

"We'll share that watch," Liz said to Hammet.

"I'll go first," Hammet said and Liz didn't argue.

"If you hear anything," Liz said, "wake me up
before you do anything."

"Sure."

She made herself as comfortable as she could, with
her saddle as a pillow, but sleep just refused to come.

"How do you stand it?" she asked.

Startled, he said, "What?"

"The cold, how do you stand it? I'd never be able
to live up here."

"You get used to it. After a while it's almost like
you don't feel it anymore."

"Jesus, to get to that point I'd have to be dead."

Briefly she thought of huddling together to combat

the cold, but he didn't seem to mind the weather and she didn't think he'd go for the idea anyway. She tried to wrap the blanket tighter and ignore the cold.

"Clay, can we talk?"

"About what?"

"About you and Al Toliver."

"I don't want to talk about him."

"Why not?"

"Because he might be dead."

"He's too stubborn to be dead, don't you think?"

There was a moment of silence and then Hammet said, "Yes. My mother always said he was the stubbornest man she ever knew. She said in that way I was like him."

"How old were you when you met him?"

"I guess I was thirteen. I never knew I had an uncle up to that point, and then he showed up. At first my mother didn't want to let him in, but he told her that all of the stories she'd heard about him weren't true, and he only wanted a chance to prove it. I didn't know what stories she meant, but I got to like him real quick."

"And then what happened?"

"And then he ran for sheriff and got elected. That changed him."

"How?"

"Well, I never did really learn what the stories about him were, but when I met him I got the impression that he wasn't like all the others around here. He'd travelled, he'd seen a lot, and I wanted to be like him . . . and then he became sheriff and settled down."

"And you don't want to do that."

"Never, especially not since I learned how good I was with a gun."

"How good? You mean fast, or accurate?"

"Both. I hit what I aim at and I hit it faster than anyone else."

"Have you ever faced a man?"

"No, but I've shot in contests and I've never been beaten. Everybody around here knows I can't be beat."

"And now you want to prove it in a show-down."

"That's right . . . and none of this, or the fact that we're riding together, is gonna change my mind. You're my ticket out of this town and after I leave here I'll be famous."

"You sure will," she agreed. "You won't have a moment's peace, because there will always be someone after you to prove that they're faster and better than you are. It gets real tiring after a while, Clay."

"Being famous? How could that get tiring? Being nobody, now there's something that can be tiring."

"Now you wait and see, Clay. Wait until the time that you wish you could crawl into a hole and pull it in after you, just for some peace and quiet."

"You're supposed to be sleeping."

"You're right, I am."

Slowly, the warmth began to increase inside the blanket and she felt herself becoming sleepy. Soon, she drifted off.

Later he woke her and she sat up, holding the blanket close, trying to keep the warmth that she'd generated. Hammet, she noticed, being used to the weather, fell asleep almost immediately.

While keeping her eyes and ears open she found

herself watching him as he slept. His face was very peaceful, and she wondered what his dreams were like. Were they filled with killing? If they were it was killing that was to be done, and not nightmares like hers of the killings already done.

It was too late for her to stop living by her gun, but maybe she'd be able to keep Hammet from starting out on that trail. Especially if Toliver died, she wanted to be able to do that for him and his nephew.

She looked up at the moon and saw a tiny sliver that was throwing off almost no light at all. If their quarry was travelling by night, they were moving very slowly. By morning, the men would be dog tired while they, on the other hand, would be well rested and able to make excellent time.

Hopefully, they'd catch up to them tomorrow and be able to head back to Clearwater.

She wondered how the sheriff was and hoped that he was still alive.

"I'm so tired I feel like I'm draggin' my ass behind me with both hands," Bull said.

"Shut up and keep riding. I'll tell you what I been thinking. That should keep you awake."

"If it's a way to get rid of this damned posse I'll stay awake to hear it."

"Remember that gang we tried to join up with before we hit Clearwater?"

"That was another one of your great ideas."

"They wouldn't let us in, right?"

"That's right."

"Why?"

"Because you had to have five hundred dollars to

buy in. I never heard of such crap, payin' to be in a gang —"

"Oh, shut up. It makes sense. Everybody in the gang puts up five hundred dollars that goes towards food and gettin' outfitted —"

"Wait a minute. Are you sayin' that we take the money we got from the bank and buy into this gang?"

"The first job we're in on, Bull," Jake said, "our share will more than make up for it."

"We only got nine hundred each, Jake."

"And I'm willing to pay five hundred of mine to get in with them."

"I don't know . . ."

"Bull, how many men are in that posse that's been trailing us?"

"I don't know."

"I'd guess that there ain't more than half a dozen, maybe less. Now how many men are there in that gang?"

"Near twenty, I reckon."

"That's right, if they haven't gotten more by now. Once we're in that gang this posse won't dare try and take us."

"Well," Bull said, grudgingly, "you have a point there."

"Damn right I do."

"But what makes you think they're gonna take us in? You remember what they said to us last time."

Indeed, Jake Pringle remembered. His ears had burned for hours afterward, but this time he was a new Jake Pringle. He'd robbed a bank and killed a sheriff, by God, and if that didn't make him good enough to join their gang, then what the hell would?

"They'll take us in," Jake said, even though he meant that they would take *him* in.

"But how are we gonna find them?"

"We came over the mountains and they were holed up in a canyon on the down side. We just go back up the same way. We'll find 'em."

"If they don't kill us on sight."

"They won't. Wait a minute. What was the name of that town at the base of the slope? Remember it?"

"Little shit town, a few old, falling-down clapboard buildings?"

"Yeah, but they had a saloon and a hotel. What was the name . . . Haven, that was it. Haven! If we can get there we'll be all right."

"If the posse don't get us first."

"They will if you go to sleep!"

"All right," Bull Benton said, "I'm up . . . I'm up!"

CHAPTER TWENTY

In the morning Liz roused Hammet, who rose with a start, staring about.

"Hey," she said. He looked at her and focused his eyes. "You all right?"

"Fine," he said, "I'm fine. Any coffee?"

"I didn't make any."

"Why the hell not?"

"I figured we should get an early start. However, if you really want coffee I could —"

"Forget it," he said, getting to his feet and collecting his gear. "Let's mount up."

While they saddled their horses Liz asked, "Did you come up with any bright ideas during the night?"

"Not a one."

"I did."

He leaned on his horse and looked at her.

"Let's hear it, then — as if I could stop you."

"See that mountain ahead?"

"How could I miss it?"

"I think they're headed for that mountain."

"What gives you this wonderful idea?"

She couldn't resist.

"Experience."

He surprised her, then.

"All right, we'll go with your experience."

"Oh . . . all right, then," she said, taken aback. "Let's get moving."

As he mounted up, though, she heard him mutter, "Older women. . . ."

Jake and Bull reached Haven by midday, and it was as they remembered it — if not worse. There were perhaps three buildings standing complete, and the rest were in various stages of falling down.

"Jesus, what a mess," Bull said.

"Yeah, so what? Let's find the saloon and ask around. We'll spend the night here and if we don't hear from the gang by morning we'll go up into the mountains and look for them."

"Easy to say. . . ." Bull muttered as they directed their horses down Haven's main street.

Just before they entered there was a sign that said: HAVEN, THE DAKOTA TERRITORY, POP. -3. The sign had been used many times for target practice and what was left was rotting away. There was barely enough room on it for the writing.

"Minus three?" Bull said.

Jake ignored him as they continued down the

street. Eventually they came to one of the still completely standing buildings that said HAVEN SALOON.

"Let's go in here. We'll have a drink, drop the word that we're looking for the gang, and then go over to the hotel and get a room."

"I hope the hotel is cheap," Bull said, dismounting. "We only have four hundred a man leeway."

The saloon was empty except for the bartender and a man sitting in the corner, nursing a beer. The man looked up as the two strangers entered and he listened while they talked. When he realized that they were asking about the gang, he spotted the sack that one of them was holding. Money was taken from the sack to pay for the drinks. He waited for the strangers to finish their drinks and leave and when the bartender nodded he went over to talk to him.

"What's their story?"

"They're looking to buy in," the bartender said.

"Do they have the money?"

"More than enough in that sack. Did you notice the writing on it?"

"Yes," the man said. "The Bank of Clearwater."

"You gonna talk to Butch?"

"Yeah, but we'll let them wait until morning and sweat. Gimme a drink for the ride."

The bartender poured the man a whiskey which he knocked back and then he went out the back way to get his horse.

George Leroy Parker, called "Butch" by the men who rode with him, was relaxing in his cabin, enjoying the charms of Lisa Dill, whose father ran the saloon down in Haven. The reason Sam Dill helped the gang out was because he thought his daughter was being held hostage. At the moment, it was Lisa who was doing the holding.

She had Parker's swollen penis held in her two hands and was working on it with her tongue and lips, licking it, getting it good and wet before she popped it into her mouth and began sucking it furiously.

"Ah, yeah, girl, that's it," Parker said, closing his eyes and grabbing her behind the head. This was Parker's favorite form of relaxation, and his men knew better than to interrupt him while he was so engaged.

Parker was barely twenty years old, but he ruled his gang with an iron hand. Men twice his age bowed to his brains and bravery, and women thought him handsome and courageous. Lisa Dill thought Parker loved her, but what he loved was the sucking motion of her mouth, her big, firm breasts and her deep, wet cunt. Beyond those things she could have been any woman.

"Jesus," Parker exclaimed as she suckled him to completion and then rocked back on her heels, licking her lips. If only she had a prettier face, he thought. Her mouth was too small and her nose too big, but she knew her business and she was only seventeen.

"How was that, Butch?"

She also needed to constantly be told how talented she was, which was sometimes a pain in the ass.

"You were fine, Lisa, just fine. Go out and let the boys know I'm ready, will you?"

"Sure, Butch."

He pulled his pants up as she went out and told

them that he was ready to hold court. Ha, hold court, just like he was "Judge" Parker instead of plain old George Leroy Parker.

More likely than not the boys in his gang were fighting among themselves and it was up to Parker to settle their disputes like Solomon. There were other women in the camp — three to service over twenty men — and he hadn't yet had to cut one of them in half to settle a dispute, but he was looking forward to the problem.

Instead of a dispute though, one of his men, Dave Tree, the half Indian, came in to talk to him.

"I thought you were in Haven," Parker said.

"I was, Butch, but I came to tell you there were a couple of fellas in the saloon asking about us."

"Lawmen?"

"No, not law. You remember them fellas came through here last week and wanted to join up until you told them they had to buy in?"

"Yeah, they bought that story didn't they?" Parker began to laugh at the memory of the looks on the faces of those men when he told them that whopper. "What a bunch of tinhorn coñ-men."

"Well, this here was two of them, and they had a sack of money marked the Bank of Clearwater. Butch, they got the money to buy in."

"Two of them, you say? There was four last time, wasn't there?"

"Yep, but there's only two now."

"Well, wait until morning and we'll bring 'em on up, Dave. This should be the easiest thousand dollars this gang ever made!"

Just the thought of easy money made him all ready

for Lisa Dill again, and he told Dave to send her back in on his way out.

His men would just have to wait for the wisdom of Solomon.

Liz Archer and Clay Hammet camped again that night when Hammet was impatient to go on. They were about three hours daylight ride from the base of that mountain. An all-night ride would have brought them there, but they wouldn't have been in any shape to take on a couple of murdering bank robbers. They had no knowledge whatsoever that a town called Haven was there waiting for them. Or what was waiting for them beyond Haven. More than they bargained for, surely.

Much more.

CHAPTER TWENTY-ONE

Jake Pringle and Bull Benton were in Haven's poor excuse for a livery, saddling their horses, when five men suddenly appeared like apparitions, effectively surrounding them.

"We ain't got any money," Bull said immediately, figuring it for a holdup.

"Ha, that's a lie," one of the men said, "I was in the saloon last night when you came in with that sack of money."

"What sack of money?"

"That sack of money," the man said, pointing to the sack that was hanging from the horn of Jake's saddle.

"You from the gang?" Jake asked.

"That's right. We heard you were looking to buy in."

"That's right," Jake said, swelling his chest. "We

held up a bank and took care of a lawman in Clear-water.''

"Took care of?'' the man asked, frowning. "What does that mean?''

"I shot him.''

"Killed him?''

"You bet.''

Dave Tree frowned. Butch wouldn't like that. He didn't want any of his men bringing unnecessary heat down on the whole gang.

"All right, you fellas mount up and follow us. We'll take you to the boss.''

"Fine,'' Jake said, exchanging a look with Bull that said, I told you so.

Bull Benton still had to be convinced.

Liz and Hammet reached Haven a scant hour after Jake and Bull had left with five gang members.

"Shit,'' Hammet said, when he saw the buildings. "Is this supposed to be a town?''

"That's what it says,'' Liz said, indicating the sign.

"Minus three,'' she said. "That must be somebody's idea of a joke.''

"This whole town looks like somebody's piss-poor idea of a joke,'' Hammet said with a sneer.

"Well, let's see if there's anybody around.''

"Maybe we can get some breakfast.''

"It would probably be a somebody's piss-poor idea of breakfast.''

He glared, but did not reply.

They rode ahead until they came to a building marked Haven Saloon.

"Think they're open this early?'' Hammet asked.

"The doors are open. Let's check."

They dismounted, secured their mounts to a rickety hitch-rail and walked inside the saloon. It was empty except for a man behind the bar who was leaning on the bar top, holding his liver-spotted bald head in his equally spotted hands.

This was Sam Dill and whenever there wasn't a gang member around he could usually be found holding his head in his hands, lamenting the absence of his sweet little girl, Lisa, who was being held in the clutches of the gang leader, George Leroy Parker.

His poor little girl.

"Hey," Hammet called.

The man's reaction startled them. He pulled his head up so fast it like to snapped off his neck, and his eyes were wide and frightened. He appeared to be a man in his mid-fifties, and his eyes were blood-shot with heavy bags underneath. He looked from Hammet to Liz and gradually relaxed.

"You ain't with the gang," he said. He'd never seen these two before, which didn't mean they weren't new members, but he didn't think the gang would be taking on any gun-toting females, and this one looked like she knew how to use the gun as well as wear it.

"What gang?" Liz asked.

The man's eyes suddenly turned wary and he said, "Never mind."

"We're looking for two men," Hammet said, "who would have ridden through here late yesterday more than likely."

"Didn't see them."

"They robbed a bank and shot a lawman in Clearwater," Liz said. "They might have been carrying a canvas sack with bank markings."

"They wasn't here."

"Why don't I believe you?" Liz asked.

"Can't help that," the man said. "They're not here."

"Where are they, then?" she asked.

"Don't know."

"You mean they were here but they're not now?" Hammet asked.

"No, they never was here."

"Look, old man —" Hammet started, reaching across the bar for the man's shirt.

"Clay —"

"This jasper's lying through his teeth. I want to see how he lies with no teeth at all."

"N-no —" the man said, leaping back away from Hammet's grasp until he banged into a shelf filled with liquor bottles, knocking one to the floor. The bottle shattered, glass and whiskey spreading out from the point where it hit.

"Mister, we don't want to hurt you —"

"I do," Hammet said.

"— but we could use your help. Maybe you could use ours, too, huh?"

"You can't help me," he said. "There aren't enough of you to help me."

"There's plenty of help right here with the two of us, Mister," Hammet said. "Believe me."

That was the nicest thing Hammet had said about Liz, and he went and ruined it with his next breath.

"This here is Liz Archer, otherwise known as Angel Eyes. You ever heard of her, mister?"

"Angel Eyes?" he asked, looking at Liz. She could see in his eyes that he recognized the name, and silently cursed Hammet for invoking it.

"She's lightning fast with a gun old man, and she ain't even the fastest of the two of us."

Hammet's contention that he was the fastest of the two failed to impress the man, but he was impressed with Liz's presence.

"Maybe there's a chance . . ." he said in a low voice.

"There's no chance if you don't talk to us, mister," Liz said.

"You're right, you're right," he said. "Would you two be hungry?"

"Some," Hammet said immediately.

"Why don't I fix you some grub and then we can talk."

"You wouldn't be planning any tricks, would you?" Hammet demanded.

"Mister, my little girl's life is on the line," the man said. "Would I risk that?"

"Maybe not."

"Have a seat and I'll bring out some food," the man said. "I've got a story to tell. . . ."

CHAPTER TWENTY-TWO

Jake and Bull followed Dave Tree, who had not introduced himself, and were flanked by the other four men. They were being escorted rather than following the group to the boss, but that suited Jake just fine. He was going to like being a member of a gang that was this careful.

They passed two points where Tree signaled to a guard and eventually entered a canyon that was sprinkled with tents and one cabin.

They were the center of attraction riding through the middle of the canyon. Men came out of the tents to look at them and from one tent came a man and a woman, both naked. The man's erection was barely noticeable beneath his overhanging belly, but the woman had large, fleshy breasts and. meaty thighs that made Jake Pringle's mouth water. She also had a handful of the man's meat, and Jake could feel his own penis swelling to fullness, making his position astride the horse a painful one.

"The women are community property," Dave Tree told him, seeing the look on his face.

"What's that mean?" Bull asked, leaning over so only Jake could hear him.

"Means anybody can have them."

The thought did not seem appealing to Bull Benton, but he was more particular than Jake Pringle in choosing his female companionship.

They stopped in front of the cabin, which was small and obviously had only one room.

"Step down," Dave Tree said. "I'll tell the boss you're here."

"Fine."

"Oh," Tree said, "how much money have you got in the sack?"

"We have the five-hundred-a-man buy in," Jake said, "don't worry."

Tree stared at the two of them. He was an imposing man with dark skin and eyes, and broad shoulders. For all his brawn Bull Benton was not a very brave man, and he said, "Eighteen hundred dollars."

Tree nodded and entered the cabin.

"You should have kept your mouth shut," Jake told Bull.

"They could have found out very easily, Jake. Why be caught in a lie?"

"That's probably the smartest thing you ever said, Bull."

Tree came out of the cabin, followed by a tall, slender man with hair the color of wheat. The man had his left arm around a small, dark-haired girl with very big breasts. His left hand held one breast so tightly that the flesh bulged.

Jake Pringle's eyes were so fixed on the girl's breasts that he barely saw the gun in the man's right hand until it went off.

The first shot struck Bull Benton in the throat, and the smartest thing he'd ever said was also the last thing he ever said.

The second shot struck a startled Jake Pringle in the forehead, taking the entire back of his head with it when it exited.

George Leroy Parker looked down at the two of them and said, "Tinhorns. Eighteen hundred dollars from a bank job. What a laugh."

"You said it, boss," Dave Tree said. He was a little startled himself, because he hadn't expected this. He had told Parker about the eighteen hundred dollars — to which the man had responded with a derisive snort — and then he told him about the dead lawman. Parker's eyes had gone cold then, and Tree probably should have suspected something at that point.

Lisa Dill started to laugh but Parker squeezed her breast so hard she gasped, instead.

"Did I tell you to laugh?"

"No, Butch."

"Then shut up."

"Yes, Butch."

He holstered his gun and told Dave Tree, "Bring the money inside, Dave. I'll divvy it up later and you can give it to the men."

"Right, Butch."

"Oh," he said, when he was halfway through the door, "and get rid of those two lumps of shit. They're stinking up our canyon."

CHAPTER TWENTY-THREE

Sam Dill introduced himself and brought Liz and Clay Hammet a feast.

"If he's trying to win us over with his cooking, he's doing a good job," Liz said.

Dill had prepared them a delicious meal of chicken and dumplings along with biscuits and pudding.

"How did you prepare this so quickly?" Liz asked him.

"I was making the biscuits and pudding anyway, but it gets pretty cold up here. I've discovered you can freeze food and it stays fresh for a long time. When you want to use it you just thaw it out and heat it up."

"But that's marvelous," Liz said. "I've never heard of that. You could make a fortune with an idea like that, especially back East."

"A fortune is no good to me without my little girl," Sam Dill said sadly.

"All right, you've made us wait long enough for this story," Hammet said. "Let's have it."

"All right. I —"

"You got any coffee?" Hammet asked, interrupting him.

"I'll get it."

Liz treated Hammet to a murderous glare while Dill was away and said, "This man has obviously suffered for a long time, Clay. Let's give him some sympathy."

"Sympathy?"

"Or at least keep your mouth shut during his story!"

"Okay, okay."

When Dill brought them the coffee Hammet immediately dunked a biscuit into it and said, "Go ahead, tell your story."

Dill's story was simple and to the point. A gang of about twenty men, led by a man named George Leroy Parker, had made their headquarters in a canyon further up the mountain some months earlier. From there they made their numerous raids on towns in the area. Soon after they had arrived they had come to Haven which at that time had a population of three, Dill, his daughter, and a liveryman, all of whom hoped in vain that Haven, once a prosperous mining town, would somehow come back to life.

During their first visit to the town Dill had fed them all at which time they had pistol-whipped him and taken his daughter.

"I've been working for them ever since."

"How?"

"The town is dead, but a lot of people pass through on their way up and down the mountain. If any of them seem prime targets for the game, or likely members, I tell one of Parker's men."

"How do you get in touch with him?"

"One of his men is usually here."

"There's no one here now," Hammet said.

"Dave Tree, one of his men, was here last night when those two men you're trailing came in."

"Then they were here!" Hammet said. "You lying —"

"Shut up, Clay!" Liz said.

Grumbling, Hammet subsided.

"Go on," Liz said.

"It's my guess that Tree took them up to the canyon this morning."

"To join the gang?"

"That's what the two men wanted."

"They probably figure they'll be safe as part of the gang," Liz said to Hammet, who nodded and dunked a biscuit.

"I don't think they'll be joining though. Not if I know Parker."

"Do you know him? Didn't you meet him just that one time?"

"Oh no. He likes to come down here every once in a while and have me cook for him."

"I don't blame him."

"Oh, he likes my cooking all right, but I think he just wants to show me my Lisa. She sits at his table with him and acts real brave, and then he leaves and takes her with him again."

A thought struck Liz about the man's daughter, but she dared not bring it up.

"Have you ever spoken to her?"

He shook his head, tears glistening in his eyes.

"I haven't heard her voice in months. He just dangles her in front of my eyes every so often. I'd like to kill him myself!"

"You may get the chance," Liz said.

"How?"

"When's the next time he'll come down to eat?" she asked.

"Not for a while, I'd wager. He was here just two weeks ago. He usually comes down once a month."

"There goes that idea," Hammet said.

"Will you help me?" Dill asked. "Will you get my Lisa back? You can do it, miss, if you're who he says you are."

"We'll do what we can."

"What —"

Liz silenced Hammet with a look and said, "Is there someplace we can sleep for the night?"

"The hotel. The keys are all there, and I try to keep the beds clean. It's all there is for me to do, and the gang sleeps there sometimes. If the beds aren't clean they . . . they beat me."

"Tough life," Hammet said, drawing another look from Liz, but they were beginning to have less and less effect on him.

"Thank you for telling us all of this," she said to the man. "We'll try and help. We'll go up there in the morning and check out the situation."

"Thank you. I'll have breakfast waiting for you in the morning."

"You needn't —"

He smiled sadly and said, "I enjoy cooking."

She nodded, and she and Hammet stood and left the saloon.

Outside he said, "You don't really intend to try and rescue that man's daughter, do you?"

"We can take a look."

"Yeah, we'll take a look and then get the hell out of here. If our boys have joined up with the gang and are holed up in a box canyon, how do you expect to get them out?"

"You're kidding, of course."

"Why?"

"I've got Wild Bill Hickok and Tate Gilmore all rolled up in one as a partner," she said. "We can do anything together, can't we?"

"Very funny. I'll bet his little daughter is up there of her own free will, servicing the whole gang. What else did she have down here?"

The same thought had struck Liz before, but she hadn't said anything then and she didn't say anything now. It irked her that she agreed with him.

"We'd better get some sleep so we can get an early start in the morning."

"After breakfast," Hammet said. "I'll give the old man that, he sure can cook."

They put their horses up in the makeshift livery behind the hotel and claimed a room each.

"Wouldn't it be safer if we shared a room?" Hammet asked, surprising Liz.

"Safer for who?" she asked. "You want to sample the merchandise before you kill me, Clay?"

"If you were real good to me, maybe I'd change my mind," he said, touching her hair.

"Not a chance, Clay Hammet," she said, pulling away from him, "Not a chance."

She went into her chosen room and slammed the door behind her, noticing as she did that the lock was broken.

He wouldn't dare. . . .

CHAPTER TWENTY-FOUR

Parker finished splitting up the money and said to Dave Tree, "All right, distribute it to the men."

"Right, Butch."

Park often thought of Tree as his "right" man, because everything he told the man to do was met with a "Right, Butch." He liked it that way. He thought that if he told Tree to put a gun to his temple and pull the trigger the man would say, "Right, Butch," and pull the trigger.

Well, almost. . . .

"When you finish with that get back down to Haven before it gets too dark to travel. I want to know if there was a posse trailing those two. Old man Dill just might get brave enough to send them up here after us."

"You should have killed him a long time ago."

Parker smiled and said, "I want to keep Lisa in an agreeable mood."

Tree couldn't blame him for that. Except for her face, Lisa was the best of the gang women, and she was Parker's exclusive property.

"Okay, Dave?"

"Right, Butch."

Grinning, Parker said, "Right," and laughed.

She heard the door open and was surprised that he would try it. She let him get close to the bed and as he bent over her she sprang up and pushed him away.

"Damn you, Hammet!" she said.

He regained his balance and said, "Don't play games with me, Liz. You fucked Al Toliver and now you've got a chance at a real man. Don't blow it."

"Real man," Liz said with contempt. "Your uncle is more man right now in his condition that you will ever be."

"Don't call him my uncle!"

"Why not? If you're not here with me because he's your uncle, then why are you here?"

"Because he was my mother's brother!"

Liz stared at him, a shape silhouetted in the dark, and said, "Could it be, Clay Hammet, that you loved someone in your life?"

"I won't talk to you about my mother!" he said, storming out of the room and slamming the door behind him.

She got out of bed, fully clothed but bootless, and considered propping a chair against the door. She decided against it. He had been rebuffed once; he wouldn't try it again.

She moved to the window to look out and just

barely caught sight of a shape moving across the street and disappearing out of sight beneath her window.

Somebody was in town, and they were entering the hotel!

Dave Tree had been across the street from the hotel when he heard the commotion inside. Two voices, a man's and a woman's, raised in some sort of argument.

A posse?

He hurried across the street and entered the hotel as quietly as he could.

Liz turned the knob of Hammet's door quietly and slipped inside. He sat in bed, peering through the darkness, and saw the glint of moonlight off her hair.

"Oh, so you changed your mind and now you want it, huh?" he sneered.

"I hope I never get that desperate," she said, whispering, "and keep your voice down."

"Why?"

"Somebody just came into the hotel."

"Who? The old man?" he asked, lowering his voice.

"I don't think so. I just got a glimpse, but it didn't look like him."

"One of the gang," he said, swinging his legs to the floor.

She nodded, even though he couldn't see it in the dark.

"He must have heard us arguing."

Hammet strapped on his gun and said, "Come on, let's get him."

"You stay up here and wait for him," she said.

"I'll go out the back and come in the front and get behind him."

"Is that an order?"

"It's a suggestion, damn it!"

"Okay, fine!"

Shaking her head she slipped from the room and moved hurriedly and quietly toward the back.

Gun drawn, Dave Tree started up the stairs to the second floor, mindful of the rickety boards he knew creaked. In the upstairs hallway he paused to listen but couldn't hear anything. Apparently whoever had been arguing had stopped.

A man of infinite patience, Tree simply stood there waiting for some sort of sound that would tell him which way to go. To his surprise, it came from behind him. . . .

Liz Archer had not been up and down the stairway of the hotel as many times as Dave Tree, so she did not know which boards creaked and which didn't. When she stepped on the first and heard the sound she stopped and held her breath. From then on she picked her steps very carefully, but one creak had been enough. . . .

Dave Tree flattened himself against the hallway wall, waiting for whoever was on the steps to come into view. None of the gang was supposed to be in town so he felt sure he could fire first and ask questions later, and that was just what he intended to do.

Clay Hammet did not have Dave Tree's patience and

finally got tired of waiting for something to happen. He drew his gun and opened his door as quietly as he could. Surprisingly, it opened as if it had been recently oiled, without a sound.

That miracle saved Liz Archer's life. . . .

Liz reached the top of the stairs, and as the man stepped out in front of her she saw the gun in his hand and heard the shot all in the same instance. There was no flash of light and no impacting of lead on any part of her body. The man at the head of steps began to fall towards her and she moved to one side to let him fall by, tumbling end over end to the bottom of the steps.

She looked up and saw Hammet standing there.

"I just saved your life," he said. "You owe me a ride in the feathers for that."

"Oh, shut up!"

Having heard the shot Sam Dill came running across the street with a shotgun in his hand. He entered the hotel lobby on the run just as Liz had lighted a lamp.

"Hey, take it easy oldtimer," Hammet told him. "The excitement's all over."

"What happened?"

"We got some company," Hammet said, indicating the man on the floor.

Liz was crouched over the fallen man, checking to make sure he was dead. Hammet had put a bullet squarely in the man's back.

"Do you know him, Sam?" she asked. Struggling, she turned the man over and then stood back so the saloon owner could get a good look.

Sam Dill came over and looked down at the man. She watched his face, just in case he decided to lie to them for some reason, but recognition was written all over it. He caught his breath and staggered back a step or two.

"That's Dave Tree," he said in awe, "Parker's right-hand man." He stared in turn at Hammet and Liz, then settled his eyes on Liz and said, "Maybe you can help me."

"Shit," Hammet said, under his breath, "I'm the one who killed him."

CHAPTER TWENTY-FIVE

They decided that they were safe for a while. If Parker had sent Dave Tree down to town at dusk, then he wouldn't be expecting him back until the following morning.

"We'll have to go up there real early," Liz said.

Having given up on sleep for the rest of the night they were in the saloon, sitting down over a cup of Sam Dill's excellent coffee. Sam was also seated there with them, whether Clay Hammet liked it or not.

"How are we going to find the place? We can't go stumbling around up there hoping to bump into it."

"Me," Sam said.

"You, what?" Hammet asked.

"I'll take you up there."

"Do you know where it is, Sam?" Liz asked.

"Well, I've never been there myself, but I've heard them talk when they come down. I could find it."

"Have you ever been up the mountain?"

"Not for many years, but the face of a mountain doesn't change much."

"He'd just slow us down," Hammet argued.

"They have two checkpoints where you'd have to get by a guard. They have a system where they communicate with each other by mirrors."

"If we can get up there early enough maybe there won't be enough sun for them to communicate," Liz said.

"That would mean leaving when it's dark," Hammet said.

"Or just before. Sam knows the way so there shouldn't be any danger of injuring the horses."

"Now you want to travel at night?" Hammet asked, exasperated.

"Not at night," she said again, "just before daybreak. What do you say, Sam?"

"I'm with you."

"Have you got a horse?" Hammet asked.

"A mule, out back."

"A mule?" Hammet asked, laughing.

"His mule will probably handle the going better than our horses," Liz said. She turned to Sam and said, "How long is it to the first checkpoint, Sam?"

"Less than an hour."

"All right, then. You'd better get ready. We'll leave in an hour."

"Right."

As the old man got up and went out Hammet said, "Look at him. He's fat and he's over fifty. He'll do nothing but slow us down."

"He's got more right to go up there than we do, Clay."

"All right, what if he's a liar? What if he's leading us into a trap?"

"All right then, stay behind."

"Just answer my question. What if he's leading us into a trap?"

"He's not," she said stubbornly.

"How do you know?"

"Because I've got something you don't."

"Oh, yeah, experience," Hammet said.

"No," Liz said, "not experience."

"Then what?"

She looked at him and said, "Woman's intuition."

It was still dark when they started up the slope, but Sam Dill moved with confidence, maybe too much confidence. Liz decided to keep an eye on him. She had the feeling he'd been up this slope more times, and more recently, then he'd let on.

CHAPTER TWENTY-SIX

They reached the first checkpoint without mishap, just as it was getting light.

"We'd better stop here," Sam said, calling their small column to a halt. "The checkpoint is just up ahead."

"You stay with the horses, Clay," Liz said, dismounting. "I'll go up ahead with Sam."

"Hey, wait a minute," Clay complained. "Why should you and he —"

"Clay, I'm getting tired of having an argument everytime I open my mouth," she hissed at him. "This partnership is dissolved and I just took charge. Now stay here and stop whining!"

He stared at her in stony silence and accepted the reins of her horse and Sam's mule. Liz knew that instead of getting through to him she was alienating him even more, but it couldn't be helped. She'd just have to deal with his resentment when the time came.

"Sam, take me up ahead."

"Come on."

They moved forward slowly and Liz wàs surprised at how light on his feet the heavy man was. He held his shotgun in one hand and used his other hand to touch a rock or a stone here and there as if he were feeling his way alone.

"You've done this before, Sam," she said, finally unable to resist.

"I wasn't always a saloon owner in a dead town," he replied. "Remind me to tell you about it when this is all over."

She'd remember.

"Okay, just up ahead. See him, up on that slate ridge?"

"He must have the balance of a billy goat," she said. "It shouldn't be too hard to knock him off of there."

"A shot would be heard."

"I wasn't thinking about shooting him off," she said. She shucked her jacket, then shocked Sam Dill by opening the top two buttons of her shirt, shrugging, and going the rest of the way. She removed the shirt and stood in the morning light naked to the waist. Her original intention had been to show enough of her breasts to catch the man's interest, but after she'd undone the second button she figured she might as well go ahead and strip, assuring herself of all his attention.

Dill stared at her full breasts and pink nipples, which were tightening from the chill in the air.

"What? . . ." he asked, unable to avert his eyes from her creamy flesh.

She looked around for a fist-sized rock, found one

and palmed it, putting her hand behind her back.

"Wish me luck."

He had another question, but she left before he could ask it.

Up on his slate perch Joe Caleb stood smugly. A lot of the men said he'd never be able to hold his balance up here, but he always was part mountain goat. He was proud of the fact that no one was able to use his spot when they stood guard.

Looking down Caleb saw the blonde-haired girl walking toward him, naked to the waist. He opened his mouth to say something, but the sight of all that flesh had struck him dumb.

It would soon strike him dead.

She walked jauntily toward the man on the ridge who spotted her almost immediately. Looking down he was able to see what she wanted him to see, and he reacted like any other man would have.

He stared.

By the time he found his tongue and said, "Hey, you —" she was close enough. She brought her hand around from behind her back and threw the rock as hard as she could. It struck the startled man in the chest, knocking him off balance. He tried to retain his upright position, but his boot heel slid off the slick, slate surface and he finally toppled off his perch to the rocks below.

She rushed to check him out, but she needn't have bothered. He'd broken both his back and his neck and was quite dead.

"Sorry, friend," she said. "I hope you enjoyed the last thing in life you saw."

She stood up and started back towards Sam Dill, buttoning her blouse as she did.

That was something Clay Hammet and no other man would have been able to do.

It had worked so well at that checkpoint that she decided to do it again at the next.

This guard was standing on firmer ground, but he was just as susceptible to naked female flesh. As she approached he actually started to bring his rifle to his shoulder and stopped short. She threw the rock and immediately felt she'd miss. She'd thrown it too high, but the man was especially tall and the rock hit him squarely between the eyes.

He was dead before he hit the ground.

"All right," she said, as Sam Dill handed her her shirt and held her jacket for her to slip into, "now we can go all the way."

A dumbfounded Clay Hammet, who had not seen her the first time she pulled the trick, said, "I thought you just did."

With the checkpoint guards out of the way Sam Dill was able to lead them right to the mouth of the gang's hideout.

"It's just up ahead," Dill said. "There'll be a guard on it."

"You gonna strip buck-naked this time and march right in?" Clay Hammet asked.

"You should be so lucky. Secure the animals and let's see how close we can get."

"Yes, boss."

She ignored his tone and the three of them began to inch their way closer. As they came to an outcropping of stones Hammet stopped short and said, "Jesus Christ."

Liz saw what he meant. Lying in a tangle on the sharp rocks were two bodies. They had apparently been thrown there, and the sharp rocks had cut them to ribbons.

Hopefully, they had been dead long before.

Sam Dill moved forward to take a look.

"Shot dead, both of them."

Liz moved forward to take a look. Their faces were covered with blood, but she was able to identify them even though she'd only seen them that one night when she played poker with them.

"It's them."

"Who?" Hammet said.

"Jake and Bull, the men we're after."

"They're dead?"

Liz took one last look at them and then turned away.

"Are they ever."

CHAPTER TWENTY-SEVEN

"That's it!"

"What's it?" Liz asked, looking at Clay Hammet.

"It's over. They're dead and we don't have to go any further."

"What about my daughter?" Sam Dill said. "What about my Lisa?"

"Your Lisa," Hammet said before Liz could stop him, "is probably in there with more dicks stuck in her than a porcupine has quills — and loving it."

Dill moved faster than Liz could have imagined. His right hand came around and exploded against Clay Hammet's chin. Hammet went staggering back and fell in a tangle on some rocks, a dull one of which struck him right on his butt, numbing his lower extremities.

"Son of a bitch!" he said, reaching for his gun.

"Clay!" Liz hissed, jumping between him and Dill. "A shot will give us away."

The sense of her statement reached him, and then so did the pain from the base of his spine.

"Jesus," he said, rolling over.

"I'm sorry," Dill said to no one in particular. "I swore I'd never hit another human being, but —"

"Swore, Sam?" Liz asked. "When?"

"Years ago, when I gave up my badge."

"Badge?"

He nodded.

"I used to be a U.S. marshal many years ago. I gave it all up when I struck a prisoner and killed him."

"Why?"

"He had killed a woman, and a crooked judge let him off. He chose to mock me and I hit him."

"And killed him."

He nodded.

"What happened?"

"I went on trial and was acquitted," he said, "by the same judge."

How ironic, she thought.

"I gave up my badge though, and became a saloon keeper. That was twenty years ago. I've never struck another person until today."

"He didn't mean it —"

"Sure he did," Dill said, "and I've thought the same thing myself. Lisa has all the makings of a tramp, Liz. Just like her mother. All she needed was someone to bring it out. Someone like Parker."

Liz stared at Dill, thinking that the man must have had a hell of a hard life.

"Sam. . . ."

"I still want her back though," he said. "I still want to save her, even if it's just from herself. Only I should have done it a long time ago myself instead of waiting for someone else to come along."

"Sam. . . ."

"Clay's right, Liz. Your job is done. Go on and leave. I'll get her out myself."

"Best advice I've heard in a while," Clay Hammet said, trying to get to his feet and wincing at the pain. "Shit, that's almost as bad as getting kicked in the balls."

"Sam," Liz said, "we're going to help you."

"You're going to help him," Hammet said. "Not me, sweetie."

"Yes, you are," Liz said, turning to face him, "Or you and me are going to take up where we left off right here and now."

Hammet stared at her, his butt aching and his hands shaking. He knew he could take her, but not right here and now, not with no crowd watching.

"Oh no you don't," he said. "Not here, not where it's only my word. I want witnesses."

"Then make up your mind, Clay."

He stared into her angel eyes and knew that she meant what she was saying. She was willing to draw on him for a fat man and his slut of a daughter.

"You're crazy," he said. "Do you know that, lady? You're stark-raving mad."

"Make up your mind," she said, "or make your move."

God, she thought, even to her own ears it sounded so melodramatic.

"All right," he said, finally. "All right, I'll help." Rubbing his butt he added, "Just let me get some feeling back in my legs."

CHAPTER TWENTY-EIGHT

"How do we play this?" Sam Dill asked. "There's three of us and twenty of them."

"They're already three short," Clay Hammet said. "We're that far ahead of them."

"Right," Liz said, glad that Hammet was thinking the right way. "Still, we can't just go waltzing in there."

"You can," Hammet said. "Just get naked."

"Any women in there, Sam?"

"Yes. They have several women who are community property."

Liz turned to Hammet and said, "One of the women would probably shoot me."

"Well, I could get naked and go with you."

"Thanks for the offer, but let's figure something else out."

"Like what?"

She thought a moment, then said, "Like a challenge."

"What kind of challenge?" Hammet asked.

"A challenge to this Parker's manhood."

"What are you talking about?"

"Come on. We've got a lot of work to do. I'll explain on the way back to town. . . ."

Working very quickly, they had their work done by midday.

Along the trail, at intervals of one hundred feet, they staked out the bodies of the gang members, using boards from some of the town buildings to prop them up. The last of the three was Dave Tree and there was a note pinned to his chest with a knife.

Parker,
I want my daughter, or you're next, coward.
                                        Sam Dill

With that done, they went back to town to prepare.

"Say that again?" Parker said. He pushed away the naked Lisa Dill as if her closeness hindered his hearing.

The man speaking was named John Teal, and he had been sent to find out what had happened to Dave Tree and the two checkpoint guards. He had found all three of them staked out down the mountain.

"They're all dead, and Tree had this note stuck to his chest with a knife."

He handed the note to George Leroy Parker, who reddened as he read it.

"The old man's gone crazy."

"Maybe," Teal said, "but he could lead the law up here to us."

"Maybe he could," Parker said, "if he was still alive. Have the boys get ready."

"Yessir."

"Butch," Lisa said in a small voice, "you can't kill my pa."

He slapped her down to the floor.

He was going to have to teach Teal how to say, "Right, Butch!"

Sam Dill was standing at the door of the saloon, from where he had a clear view of the main street as it joined the path up the mountain.

"This is nuts," Clay Hammet said.

"Well, you said I was crazy."

They were each checking their rifles and handguns to make sure they wouldn't jam at a crucial moment. Sam Dill was armed with his scattergun, and Liz's father's old Walker Colt, which she still carried and cared for.

"What chance have we got?"

"They're expecting to come down here and face one gun," she said, "and they're going to find three. That gives us three times as good a chance as we might have."

"Lady, your arithmetic stinks."

"I never was very good in school."

"This is a good time to tell us."

"If they're coming they should be here soon," Sam Dill said.

This was a different Sam Dill talking. As soon as he had accepted the fact that he wasn't going to get out of this mess without killing some people, it was as if the saloon owner died and the marshal came back.

Even Hammet noticed the difference, although he made no mention of it.

"We'd better get into position," Liz said.

"There's three roofs in the whole town, and we're gonna use all three," Hammet said. "Where do we go from there, after they spot us?"

"Wherever we have to go to stay alive," Sam Dill said.

"Right, Sam," Liz said.

"You're both crazy."

"And you're right here with us."

"Don't forget you forced me into this."

"Wait a minute."

"What?"

"I've got an idea."

Hammet looked at Dill and said, "Now she gets an idea? When we're minutes away from facing twenty guns? I'm glad this is such a well-thought-out plan of action."

"What's the idea?" Dill asked.

"It's based on what Clay just said about where we go after the rooftops," she said, and then went on to explain what had only just occurred to her.

"That'll work," Dill said.

"Fuck it will," Hammet said.

Liz shook her head and said, "That kind of language is just never going to catch on."

"Not with me," Dill said. "I'm just too old-fashioned."

"Excuse me for beating a dead horse here," Hammet said, "but you've both lost your minds. I know I keep saying that, but you both really expect to come out of this alive."

"It's all in the attitude, Clay," Liz said.

"Yeah," he said, nodding his head, "just like your goddamn arithmetic."

Liz took her position on the roof of the hotel, with Dill on the roof of his saloon across from her, and Hammet on the partially collapsed roof of the general store to her left. She could see Hammet from where she was and he looked distinctly unhappy.

Well, she wasn't all that pleased herself.

As the time crept towards evening she started to wonder if she'd made any mistakes — aside from the obvious one of getting involved. She marveled at how she had entered Clearwater looking for some peace and quiet, and ended up on the roof of a building in a dead town waiting to take on a gang of twenty men with only two other people to help her.

That's minding your own damn business, all right. . . .

CHAPTER TWENTY-NINE

She heard it before she saw them, the sound of multiple hoofbeats as the riders approached town. Picking up her rifle she leaned on the edge of the roof and looked over at Hammet and Dill. They had both heard and were ready.

As soon as the riders came into view, Liz realized the big mistake they had made. . . .

The gang was being led by John Teal, and he felt that a great responsibility had been bestowed on him.

"Are you going to respond to the note?" he had asked Parker.

"No," Parker had said, "you are."

"But . . . he called you a coward."

"I'm a lot younger than you, Teal, but I've learned that it takes more courage to ignore a taunt or a challenge than it does to accept it. It also takes more brains."

Teal wasn't sure he understood, but Parker was the boss. That much he did understand.

"Take eight men," Parker said. "Go down to Haven, kill Dill and burn the town down. Then come back. It's as simple as that."

Teal nodded and backed out of the cabin. Eight men was almost half their force, but since they were only going down to face one man he never thought twice about it.

Inside the cabin Parker wondered if he could time their appearance in Haven so that he'd be fucking Lisa Dill when Sam Dill was being killed.

There were only nine of them!

That was the good news and the bad news. She could see that Dill and Hammet were perplexed as well, but then why should it be a surprise? Why should they have expected Parker to come to town with his entire force just to face one man?

As the nine men entered the town they were talking among themselves, laughing and shouting, and they did not expect what happened next.

As agreed Liz fired first, and she chose the man in the lead as her target. From Dill's description she did not believe him to be George Leroy Parker, but he did seem to be the leader so she took him from his horse first.

It went very quickly because they were methodical about it. The nine men were sitting ducks. She had levered another round and fired again even before the first man hit the ground, and then she heard Hammet fire his rifle and Dill his shotgun.

Hammet's shot cleanly jerked a man from his saddle, and Dill's double-O blast spread out and brought two more men to the ground. He used Liz's Walker Colt to kill them where they sat, then knocked a third man from his saddle.

Liz and Hammet levered and fired and suddenly there was silence as the bodies of nine men — all of whom had been shocked and startled and unsure as to how to react — littered the streets.

Of course it would not have been that easy if Parker had come with his entire force. They couldn't have fired quickly enough to kill twenty men, and they would have had Parker's leadership to contend with. No, if Parker had come with the entire gang, they probably wouldn't even have gotten nine of them as they just had.

Liz, Hammet, and Dill met in the middle of the street, reloading as they walked to inspect the bodies.

"Okay," Hammet said, "new plan. There's still a gang up there, even though it's smaller than it was. How do we get them out of there? I don't think the same trick is gonna work."

"Sam, is Parker here?" Liz asked.

Dill inspected the dead and then shook his head.

"He's not here."

"No, he was too smart for that," Liz said. "Too smart to react to a challenge."

"What do we do now?" Hammet asked.

"We'll have to go up after them," Liz said.

"What?"

"And catch them by surprise."

"We can't —"

"In the dark."

"You're —"

"If you say crazy again," Dill said, "I'll shoot you where we stand and take a chance that we can take the rest of them without you."

"Without me?" Hammet said. "What kind of a chance do you have with me? We have no idea how many of them are still up there. There could be twenty, thirty —"

"No," Dill said, "there was never more than twenty, twenty-five men in the gang at one time."

"All right, simple subtraction," Liz said. "Take the maximum, twenty-five. We've got nine here and three on the mountain. We've cut their force in half."

"Half is worth the whole when you're facing them on their home ground," Hammet said.

"That's why they'll be surprised," Liz said. "They won't expect us to come in after them, and they still don't know how many of us there are."

"I see," Hammet said. "From your point of view we have the advantage. Why don't we send them a note telling them there's only three of us. I mean, let's give the poor outnumbered bastards a fighting chance."

"You're starting to bore me, Clay," Liz said.

Hammet looked at Dill — surely another man would understand — but Dill just jerked his head once and said, "Me, too."

"Jesus Christ," Hammet said, following them, "all I wanted to do was kill one little female. How did I get involved with this?"

CHAPTER THIRTY

As darkness started to fall George Leroy Parker admitted something to himself.

His men weren't coming back.

"Shit!" he said, and stepped outside. To the first man he saw he said, "Get me Ranny Helm."

"I think he took one of the gals into a tent. . . ."

"I don't care if his dick is in to the hilt, tell him I want him!"

"Yessir!"

He went back inside and slammed the door.

What the hell was going on? Had fat Sam Dill managed to kill twelve of his men singlehandedly? That didn't figure. The only thing that did figure was that those two tinhorns had brought a posse up here and now they were methodically destroying his gang.

He had to get out and head for Brown's Hole like he'd always wanted to. Brown's Hole was a region that touched Colorado, Utah and Arizona. Brown's Hole was legendary. It was said that all the great gangs were holed up there and that no posse could find a gang that was hiding out in Brown's Hole. That's where he wanted to go, but first he needed a diversion.

There was a knock on the door and he called out, "Come in."

Ranny Helm walked in, hair tousled, tucking his shirt into his pants.

"You got your dick in your pants, Ranny?"

"Sure, Butch."

"Then listen, good. . . ."

Once again they rode up the slope with Dill and his mule in the lead. This time, however, it was totally dark except for a sliver of moon which was barely any help at all.

Their plan was this: they'd play it by ear and hope to have one by the time they reached the gang's hideout.

"Okay," Liz said when they reached the point where Jake and Bull's bodies were. They knew it because they could smell them. "Let's leave the animals here."

"What's our plan, boss?" Hammet asked, his tone mocking, but it was mild compared to the complaints he'd been voicing all day. Apparently he'd decided that if they were going to go ahead and do it he'd better stop fighting them and string along. Liz liked him a lot better that way.

"Can we climb in, Sam?"

"The canyon is like a hole in the mountainside,

Liz. We could probably get up to the top at any point, but it would take all night to climb down the inside walls.''

"We've got to go right in the front then.''

Hammet made a sound in his throat, but kept his mouth closed.

"How do we do that?'' he asked a moment later.

"I don't know. If we had some dynamite. . . .''

"Um, we do," Dill said.

"What?"

"I didn't want to say anything because I didn't want to make you nervous.''

"You've been lugging dynamite up this mountain on that mule?'' Hammet asked.

"Yes,'' Dill said, "both times.''

"How much?'' Liz asked.

"A half-a-dozen sticks. It's old stuff. I don't even know if it still works, but I've got the caps and everything.''

"Do you know how to use it?''

"Yes.''

"Sam, I should kiss you,'' she said.

"Wait a minute,'' Hammet said. "I just have one question here.''

"Which is?'' Liz asked, hoping that he wasn't reverting to form.

"If we use dynamite on that entrance, what's to say we don't end up closing it, trapping us outside and them, including Dill's daughter, inside?''

Liz looked at Dill and said, "He has a point. What we'll have to do is use the dynamite as a diversion.''

"How?'' Dill asked.

"You said you could get up above the canyon hole?"

"Sure."

"Could you use the dynamite to bring down part of a wall?"

"Sure I could."

"That wouldn't just get us in," Hammet said, "it might even chase some of them out."

"Well, if they do come out," Liz said, "let them go."

"Could I say something else, here?"

"If it makes sense."

"If we let them run and we run in, then we'll be on the inside and they'll be on the outside."

Damned if he wasn't starting to make sense.

"What do you suggest?" Liz asked.

"If any of them want out before we get in, we'll have to kill them. We can't just switch places with them, Liz. That won't accomplish anything."

"You're right," she said. "That's the way we'll do it. Sam, how long will it take you to get into position?"

"Well, if I take the nearest wall I ought to be able to get into position within the hour. Give me a full hour to make sure."

"All right," she said. "I just hope nothing happens before then."

"Me too," Hammet said.

Liz waited for a further remark, but when none was forthcoming she told Dill, "Let's get to it then."

When Dill was ready to ride Hammet asked a question.

"What's our signal gonna be?"

"When the left wall of that canyon comes down with a bang," said Sam Dill, "that'll be signal enough."

CHAPTER THIRTY-ONE

An hour and five minutes later there was a huge explosion and the mouth of the canyon lit up momentarily.

Liz and Hammet had been lounging on a rock from a point where they could see the canyon mouth, but the guard there could not see them. Now that there was a flash of light they could see the guard silhouetted against it, his back to them as he stared into the canyon wondering what the hell was going on. They both drew and fired at the same time, while there was still a glow, and the man went down.

"Let's move," Liz said.

As they approached the entrance the sound of the explosion died down, but there was a rumbling like thunder in the distance.

"Jesus Christ," Hammet said, "he must have used all six sticks."

"I hope he's all right."

Concern over Dill dissolved however, as they entered the canyon, stepping over the dead man's body. Immediately someone began to fire at them and they both went sprawling in opposite directions.

The bastards were waiting for them!

Parker had set his diversion up very carefully.

He told Ranny Helm that they were going to have some visitors pretty soon, probably during the night.

"Who'd be dumb enough to try and take us at night?"

"Shut up and listen to me. Whoever it is was smart enough to kill Dave Tree, John Teal and ten other men."

"Jesus."

"We're gonna be waiting for them, though. In fact, Ranny, I'm gonna go out and lead them here."

"Butch, you can't —"

"I have to. I want you and the men to be ready. They'll try to come right through the front because there ain't no other way. As soon as they do you'll be waiting to cut them down."

"What about you?"

"I'll lead them to the canyon entrance and try to get them to come through. If you see me first, of course you won't fire," Butch said.

"Of course not."

Yeah, you son of a bitch, Butch thought, you'll probably fire at the first man you see, but that's all right because it won't be me. I'll be long gone on my way to Brown's Hole with most of the money. If you

163

think I'm going out there to risk myself, you're nuts. . . .

"I'm counting on you, Ranny."

"I won't let you down, Butch."

Just keep the bastards busy enough for me to get far away, Ranny, he thought. That's all I ask. Old Butch'll be proud of you . . . you dumb sonofabitch!

Ranny Helm almost jumped out of his skin when he heard the explosion. He and the other men looked up and what they saw froze their blood. The whole damned mountainside looked like it was coming down on them.

When Liz and Hammet came through the entrance it was only Ranny Helm who noticed them and fired. As they rolled away and the glow that had lit up the canyon faded, Ranny lost sight of them.

"Come on, men," he called, but the men were already running towards the canyon mouth. In the dark they had no idea just how much of the canyon walls were coming down, and they didn't want to wait to find out.

There were torches erected towards the center of the canyon where the tents were, but the light didn't reach beyond there. Horses had broken loose and were whinnying madly and running around the canyon in the dark. Liz couldn't see the dust, but she knew the canyon was full of it, making breathing a problem. Some of the men who were running to get out ended up being trampled by the horses. Others ran into lead being fed them by Liz Archer and Clay Hammet, who fired towards the sound of running feet.

As the sounds of the falling canyon wall subsided and the horses all found their way out, an eerie silence came over the area. Liz and Hammet stood and from where they were they could hear a man moan or a woman cry, but beyond that there was nothing.

"Clay?" Liz called.

"Here."

They found each other and she asked, "Are you all right?"

"Fine. You?"

"In one piece. They were waiting for us."

"Looks like Parker figured us out."

"But they panicked," she said. "Jesus, the horses killed half of them."

"Better move carefully. There still might be some around."

"Let's move towards the light."

They started walking towards the centre of the canyon to the tents and torches, reloading as they walked. They saw several women sitting on the ground in the light, so panicked that they hadn't known where to run so they had simply frozen where they were.

As they walked through, the women reached for them and asked for help.

"What happened?" one asked.

"It's the end of the world," another said.

"Only as you know it," Liz replied. "Are any of you Lisa Dill?"

They didn't answer so Hammet reached down and grabbed one by the shoulders.

"Are you Lisa Dill?"

The woman looked at him wild-eyed and said, "The cabin, in the cabin."

"Where's the cabin?"

The woman pointed and Liz realized that she was pointing towards the left wall of the canyon.

"Jesus," she said, and started running. Hammet grabbed a torch and followed.

The cabin was there amidst the rubble. There was just enough pieces of wood and a pipe chimney to tell them that the wall had totally flattened the cabin — and anyone who might have been in it.

"Jesus," Hammet said, "are we gonna tell Dill that he killed his own daughter?"

"If she was in there," Liz said. "Come on, let's look around."

They tripped over her about fifty feet from the cabin. Apparently she had either been outside or had run outside when she heard the noise. She was unconscious. Hammet held the torch over her, but Liz could find no serious injuries.

Eventually the girl came to and stared at them.

"Lisa?" Liz asked. "Lisa Dill?"

"Y-yes," the girl said, frowning.

Liz got up and reached down to help the girl to her feet.

"Come on, Lisa. Your father's waiting for you."

If he was alive.

They camped outside the canyon, waiting to see if Sam Dill would come down from the mountain. There was a possibility that he had been caught in his own blast. He did say the dynamite was old, but. . . .

Two hours after the blast someone approached their campfire and called out for permission to enter.

"Come ahead," Liz said, her hand on her gun.

Sam Dill came walking into the circle of their light, leading his mule, and said, "Got any coffee for a weary traveller?"

"Sure," Liz said, "and we've got something else for you too."

Dill saw his daughter then, wrapped in a blanket and slightly in shock. He approached her and she looked up at him.

"Poppa?" she said.

"Hello, baby."

"Poppa," she said again. Her arms came out from beneath the blanket and he crouched down to take her in his own.

As they hugged each other and cried, Hammet leaned over to Liz and said, "I wonder how many of those dead men she fucked?"

She looked at him in distaste and said, "You just had to go back to being a horse's ass, didn't you?"

They had left the other women in the canyon by the tents, and when daylight came they went back inside. There were three women there and they were all dead.

"Jesus," Hammet said.

They had either killed themselves, or each other, or some combination of the two. It was enough that they were dead and Liz was glad they had taken Lisa Dill out when they did.

"What made them do that?"

"One of them asked during the night if it was the end of the world," Liz said. "Maybe for them it was. Who knows what servicing all of these outlaws for who knows how long did to their minds."

Hammet gave Sam and Lisa Dill a pointed look as Sam led her away.

"She's younger than them," Liz said, gesturing to the women on the ground, none of whom had been under thirty. "She'll survive."

"If you say so," Hammet said. "Hey, Sam."

"Yes?"

"Check out them bodies and see if any of them is Parker, will you?"

Sam waved, left Lisa standing alone, and checked each body in turn. When he was finished he looked at them and shrugged, indicating that George Leroy Parker was not among the dead.

"Well," Hammet said, "he's either underneath that rubble, or he's gone."

"I say he's gone," Liz said. "He saw the end and was smart enough to get out."

"Leaving all of his men behind?"

"He was smart, we know that already. He used them as a diversion. By now he's in another state, and who knows what he'll become there."

"Then I guess it's time for us to get on back, huh?" Hammet asked.

"I guess so."

They exchanged a glance and then Clay Hammet walked back towards the Dills.

It was unspoken what was waiting for them back in Clearwater. Neither of them had to say it. It would become very clear once they got there.

Liz thought briefly, very briefly, of running to avoid the showdown, but there were a couple of reasons why she couldn't do that.

One was that Blossom was in Clearwater, and she loved that mare. She had to go back for her.

The other reason was that if she ran this time, she'd have to run the next time, and the time after that. As it stood she was a target for young men like Clay Hammet as well as the old ones. If it got around that she had run, they'd come for her in droves.

No, this had to be done one way or another.

It was now unavoidable.

CHAPTER THIRTY-TWO

Four tired, bedraggled figures rode down the main street of Clearwater some four days later. Sam Dill had decided that he and Lisa would accompany Liz and Hammet back to Clearwater, either to start a new life there or simply to use it as a jumping off point.

When Liz asked Dill if he'd consider going back to law work he shook his head and said, "I'm too old, Liz. It took me twice as long to get down that mountain after I set the charges as it did to get up. I'll probably stay in the saloon or restaurant business somewhere. I used to be a good lawman, but right now all I am is a good cook."

"Finally," Clay Hammet had said, "something that we agree on."

Now as they entered Clearwater, the fate of all four was somewhat in the air.

The Dills didn't know where they would be in the future or what they would be doing.

Liz Archer and Clay Hammet knew that they had an appointment only one of them would walk away from.

They rode to the livery where Liz turned "Tate", tired but perfectly sound, over to a jubilant Jed.

"Did you catch them?" Jed asked.

"They got caught and killed," Liz said. "That's all that matters. How's the sheriff?"

"You better talk to Doc about that."

"I'll see him after I go to the bank."

"You got the money back?"

"Some of it," she said.

They had gone through the tents and the pockets of the dead men and had come up with nearly eleven-hundred dollars. At that point they didn't know how much the bank was missing, and did not count that as much of a recovery.

"Jed, these are the Dills. Will you take care of their animals?"

Sam Dill had left the mule behind, and he and Lisa were riding two of the outlaws' horses that Liz and Hammet had been able to chase down.

"Sure thing, Miss Liz. It's nice to see you back."

"Thank you, Jed."

As she started to leave the livery Clay Hammet fell in alongside her.

"Where are you going?" she asked.

"With you to the bank. There might be a reward for the recovery of that money."

She just shook her head and kept walking.

When they reached the bank they learned the true

amount that had been stolen from the bank manager.

"Of course I did not give them the real money," he said. "I gave them eighteen hundred dollars that we keep aside just for situations like this."

Liz stared at the man and said, "It would have been nice if the sheriff had known that he was risking his life for money you were virtually giving away."

"Well," the man said lamely, "there wasn't time."

"If you had explained your ploy to the sheriff beforehand he would have known," Liz said.

"Yes, well, ah, what happened was unfortunate, I suppose. . . ."

"Yes, I suppose that's the word," she said and turned on her heel.

"Uh, miss —"

"Yes?"

"The, ah, money," the manager said, indicating the bag in her hand.

"What money?"

"Why, the bank's money?"

"Oh, that? That's all gone."

"But, the bag —"

"This is loot, Mr. Bank Manager. You wouldn't want to soil your hands with loot, would you?"

The man was speechless and Liz said, "No, I didn't think you would."

Outside Clay Hammet, who surprisingly enough had remained silent the whole time they were in the bank, asked her, "What are you going to do with the loot, Liz?"

"This?" she asked. She shoved the bag at him and said, "Here, you take it."

"Me?" he asked, his eyes narrowing suspiciously.

"I don't want it."

"Oh, I get it," Hammet said. "You're trying to buy me off."

"What?"

"You think I'll let you live for eleven hundred dollars."

"What an ass you are," she said, quickening her pace to get away from him.

He followed her though, all the way to the doctor's office.

"You're back," the doctor said as they entered. He lowered his head so he could look at them over the rim of his glasses. "Are you in one piece?"

"Yes," Liz said.

"Both of us."

Liz frowned at Hammet and then asked the doctor, "How's the sheriff."

"He died," the doctor said, "an hour after you left town. I'm sorry."

"Died?" Liz said.

"Yes. I'm sorry."

"Did he regain consciousness?"

"No, he did not. He went in his sleep."

Liz didn't know that Hammet had left until she heard the door shut behind him.

"What happened out there?" the doctor asked.

"I'm sorry?"

"I asked what happened? Did you catch them. Did you get the bank's money back?"

"Yes," she said, "yes we caught them, and no, the bank didn't want their money back."

"You mean you recovered it and they didn't want it back?"

"The bank manager is a very generous man," Liz said, holding the bag of money out to the doctor.

"What's this?"

"Eleven-hundred dollars. Use it to bury the sheriff," she said, and then when she realized that Al Toliver would already have been buried she said, "Or do whatever you can with it. It doesn't belong to anyone."

"Whatever I can?" he said, not understanding.

"Donate it to charity, use it for medical research. Just make sure it's put to good use. Since the sheriff died for it, I think he'd prefer that. Don't you?"

"I suppose . . . yes, I think he would."

"I've got to put this badge back in the sheriff's office. Is it locked up?"

"Uh, no, there is someone there temporarily."

"The town appointed someone?"

"No, a stranger is wearing the badge, a friend of the sheriff's who came into town shortly after he died. He volunteered and the town council took him up on it."

"I see."

"His name is —"

"That's all right, Doc," she said, stopping him. "I have a feeling I know who it is."

CHAPTER THIRTY-THREE

When she entered the sheriff's office he looked up from the desk but did not smile. She was elated at seeing him — her heart was pounding — but she did not smile, either. It was not the time for smiling.

"Liz," he said, getting to his feet.

"Hello, Tate. It's been a long time."

"Too long," he said. He moved toward her and took her in his arms. It surprised and pleased her. He was not normally a demonstrative man. Maybe he was just truly glad to see her.

Tate was a tall man, deceptively built along lean lines, but she knew the strength that was in that slender frame. He hadn't aged much since she saw him last, and although in his early forties he carried his years very well.

They stood that way for a few seconds, her arms encircling his waist, and she took in the feel and smell of him. She wished it could go on this way for a long time, that she could just melt into his arms and let him take care of her, but he wouldn't have wanted it that way and neither would she.

She was Angel Eyes, like it or not, and if she ever complained about it he would be right there to say I-told-you-so.

"I have a room," she said, hoping that the hotel had saved it for her.

"Good," he said, taking her arm and leading her towards the door.

Sex with Tate was different. It had to be, with a man you loved. With others it was fun, nice, even pleasurable, but with someone you loved it was . . . special.

He kissed her lips and removed her clothes as soon as they entered her room. He lingered over her breasts for a long time, using his hands and mouth, then lowered her to the bed and undressed.

They explored each other for what seemed an interminable time, the way people who haven't seen each other for a long time will talk incessantly to catch up. Liz and Tate couldn't afford to talk away valuable time, not with the kind of lives they led. If there was time for talk later they would do it, but this was the time for touching, for making contact in a way only people who love each other can.

She opened herself to him and he slid into her. She clutched his buttocks, happy that he was here with her so soon after they had both lost a friend, he an old one and she a new one.

He was tender with her, taking her in long, slow

strokes until they both approached climax, then he increased his tempo and she came moments before he did — for that one intense moment completely and totally happy. . . .

"I'm sorry about your friend," she said.

"I haven't seen him in years, but I feel such a sense of loss."

"He was a special man."

"He was that," Tate said. "He got out of this," he said, reaching up to the headboard where both their guns were hanging and slapping his gun to indicate what "this" was. "That made him special, and it made him smart."

"Yes."

"How about you? Are you all right?"

"I'm fine. Tired, but fine."

"I hear you might have some trouble here."

"You heard? Is that why you're here?"

"I wasn't far away and I heard the stories about you coming here and an itchy kid waiting for you."

"Did you come to save me, or the itchy kid?" Her tone was testy. Did he think she couldn't handle herself? He knew better than that.

"I came," he said, "to keep you from matching leather with Al Toliver. I knew he wouldn't stand for gunplay in his town. Before he allowed that he'd step in himself."

"He told me he used to make his way with a gun."

"He was one of the best, Liz. Probably still was."

"Who did you come to save, Tate?"

"You," he said. "I came to save you from killing Toliver, or from getting killed. Still amounts to you." He looked at her then and said frankly, "I'm not sure who would have won, Liz, and I wanted to get here before it happened. As it turns out, I was too late to do any good."

"He was that good?"

Tate nodded gravely.

"What about this kid?" Tate said, switching the subject.

She explained about Clay Hammet and he listened patiently to her whole story, which included an explanation of the Dills.

"Sam Dill," he said.

"You've heard of him."

"Not for a long time. I thought he was dead."

"Maybe he was. . . ."

"Do you think you got through to Hammet?"

"No, I don't. I don't think anyone could, Tate. He's too far gone. I don't see how he could be blood related to Al Toliver. He's got such an *attitude*."

"You'll have to face him, then."

"I suppose."

"Do —" he started, but that was as far as his offer got. He knew she wouldn't want him to step in. It would have been different with her and Toliver; he would have been stepping between two of his friends.

This was different.

"I'll leave the badge with you," she said.

"When will you see Hammet?"

"Soon, I guess. I gave him the badge he's wearing and I'll have to get it back. I think he knows that."

"Probably does."

"How long will you be here, Tate?"

"Not long. I was really just waiting for you. We can leave together if you like . . . after."

"I'd like that," she said, turning into his arms.
"I'd like that a lot. . . ."

They made love again, this time with more urgency.
Neither of them knew how long this time together
would have to last them until the next.

Later there was a pounding on the door, a quick and
urgent banging followed by a high voice touched with
panic.

It was Lisa Dill's voice.

"Miss Archer, oh Miss Archer."

Liz hurried out of bed and grabbed something to
cover herself with. She opened the door a crack and
looked out at Lisa's tear-stained face.

"What's wrong, Lisa?"

"It's Poppa," she said. "He's going after Clay
Hammet. He says he owes it to you."

"Damn," Liz said.

As she and Tate dressed hurriedly he asked, "Is the
kid any good, Liz?"

"I don't know, damnit," she said. "I just don't
know."

CHAPTER THIRTY-FOUR

As Liz and Tate ran from the hotel they didn't know where Hammet and Dill were, but they discovered that they did not have far to look. Farther down the street, in front of Metzger's Saloon, they could see the portly figure of Sam Dill, his back to them, his shotgun held at his side.

"Come on," Liz said, "we've got to stop them."

She sprinted ahead of Tate, but he caught up to her in sure, long-legged strides and grabbed her arm just as she was reaching Dill.

"Come over here," he said, pulling her off to the side.

"But this is my fight, not his," she insisted.

Hammet was in the street, facing the older man, and he spotted Liz.

"Sending old men in to do your fighting for you, huh, Angel Eyes?"

"I'm fighting my own fight, sonny," Dill called out to the kid.

"What did I do to you?" Hammet asked.

"You said some nasty things about my daughter," Dill said, just as Lisa caught up with Liz and Tate.

"Poppa, no —" Lisa said. Tate grabbed her as she started to run towards her father.

"He's drunk, Tate," Liz said, looking at Hammet.

"I know," Tate said, "but look at him. He's drunk and it's making him better, more sure of himself. Some people are like that, Liz. They lose their inhibitions and fears when they're drunk. There's no stopping them when they're that way. That's the way this kid is."

"We've got to stop them."

"Neither of them would thank you for that," Tate said. "Sam needs this almost as badly as the kid does."

And so they watched Dill stand with his shotgun held at his side, and a drunken Clay Hammet standing easy with a grin on his face.

Sam Dill made the first move and Hammet cleared leather before he could raise his shotgun. The kid had seen Dill flex.

Like the good ones, Tate thought.

Both Tate and Lisa Dill rushed to the fallen Sam Dill as Liz stepped out into the street to meet Clay Hammet.

When they reached him Dill looked up at Tate and said, "Tate," as if they were meeting at a church social. He was clutching his side where Hammet's bullet had caught him.

"Sam," Tate said, crouching down next to him. "Damn fool thing to do."

"I reckon."

Tate moved Dill's hand so he could examine the wound.

"How is he?" Lisa asked, her voice shaking.

"He'll be fine. Come on, Sam. Let's get you off the street."

Tate helped him to his feet and walked him off to the sidelines, sitting him in an empty chair. He took a bandana out of his pocket and slid it inside Dill's shirt.

"Hold this there."

"Yeah," Dill said, wincing at the pain. "I forgot how much it hurts to get shot."

"It doesn't change, Sam."

They all looked into the street now where Liz stood facing Clay Hammet, who, flushed from his success, was even more confident now.

"The kid's good, Tate."

"I know," Tate said, watching through narrowed eyes, "I saw."

"You gonna help her?"

"Did I help you?"

"Is she any good, Tate?" Sam Dill said. "Does she live up to her rep?"

"Do any of us?"

"Shit," Dill said, "I hope she does."

Liz saw the grin on Clay Hammet's face and the crazy, drunken glint in his eyes. Could she reason with him?

"Clay, I'll say it again. This is no good."

"This is fine, Liz," Hammet argued. "This is just where I want to be."

"Your uncle —"

"I told you not to call him my uncle!" Hammet shrieked at her. "He was just some old man who got himself killed."

"Clay —"

"I'm through talking, Liz," Clay Hammet said, "and you're all through living."

Liz reached up and took the orange bandana out from inside her shirt.

This time Hammet made the first move, which meant he was already making a concession to Angel Eyes.

Liz watched his hand as it swooped down towards his gun. She could see it very clearly. She could see that he was fast, but not as fast as she was.

She knew Tate was watching, and if she tried to wing Hammet and missed, she'd never hear the end of it.

Especially if she missed and got killed.

No, Clay Hammet was going for the kill. She had no choice but to do the same.

Tate Gilmore watched with a mixture of sadness and pride.

Sadness because a woman as beautiful, loving, and loyal as Liz Archer had to live her life as Angel Eyes. Pride because he had taught her, and as good as Clay Hammet was, she took him very easily.

Imagine, he thought, feeling pride in watching one human being gun down and kill another.

Would the world always be this sad?